# HUMAN CONDITION:

# *CRITICAL*

## LUC DE SCHEPPER
### M.D., Ph.D., Lic.Ac., C. Hom., D.I.Hom.

**PUBLISHING**

Full of Life Publishing
500 N. Guadalupe St., G441
Santa Fe, NM 87501

Other books by the same author:

"Acupuncture for the Practitioner," 1985

"Candida, the Causes, the Symptoms, the Cure," 1986

"Peak Immunity," 1989

"Full of Life," 1991

"How to Dine Like the Devil and Feel Like a Saint," 1993

Library of Congress Catalog Card number: 93-070915


ISBN 0-942501-00-4


Printed in the United States of America


Full of Life Publishing, Santa Fe, NM 87501

Note to Reader and Disclaimer

The information in this book is presented for information purposes only. All therapies, treatments, exercises or energetic interventions of any nature should be undertaken only under the direct guidance and care of a properly and legally, fully trained health care professional specializing in the services rendered. Nothing described in this book should be construed by any reader or other person to be a diagnosis or treatment for any disease or condition. Neither the author nor publisher can accept any responsibility for any ill effects resulting from the use or misuse of the information contained herein. Any uses or misuses of the information presented here for educational and entertainment purposes are the sole responsibility of the reader.

Cover and drawings designed by Yolanda De Schepper

Dedicated to my children
Peter, Isabelle, Steven, Sebastian and Luc

# ACKNOWLEDGMENTS

I could not have written this book without the help and understanding from all my patients who have entrusted their care to me. I am greatly indebted to them. I want to thank my good friends Ted Rifkin and Ken DeSure, D.C. for reading the manuscript and giving me their invaluable and thoughtful insight. I owe a lot to my teacher Robin Murphy, N.D. who has strengthened my love for homeopathy. His generosity in sharing his knowledge is a trademark of only great teachers. Many thanks to my patients and friends Bill Blankenship, Kate Noonan and Marjorie Buettell for reading the manuscript and helping me in the most positive way. As usual, it was a pleasure to work with a professional like my editor Gretchen Henkel. And most important, without the support and artistic talents of my beloved wife Yolanda, this book would not have been possible.

Luc De Schepper M.D., Ph.D., Lic.Ac., C.Hom., D.I.Hom.
New School   Homeopathy        41
5A  Lancaster  St.
Cambridge,  MA  02140
617-547-8500
www.LMhomeopathy.com

FULL  OF  LIFE  PUBL.
PO  BOX  31025
SANTA  FE,  NM  87594
FAX    505-982-4011

Tel. (714) 454-8077

"In an Art Preservative of
Life, Negligence in Learning
is  Criminal"

# TABLE OF CONTENTS

# INTRODUCTION

As we are nearing the end of the 20th Century, modern science is exploring many new ideas that could take the healing arts to new frontiers. A "bionic body," composed of neural prosthetics, could restore muscle contractions in people who are paralyzed. Implants of fetal cell material for diseases such as Parkinson's deliver a message of hope. There is hope that harvesting organisms such as sponges and coral from the relatively untouched seas could isolate active agents to prevent and cure diseases, from arthritis to cancer.

Yet the news on the medical front is not all good. Here is just a sampling of the headlines we've all grown accustomed to seeing: "Neglected for Years, TB is Back with Strains that are Deadlier" (*New York Times*, October 1992); "Official Scramble to Deal With Resurgence of Tuberculosis" (*Los Angeles Times*, July 1992); "Asthma Strengthens Its Grip, Especially Among Young" (*Los Angeles Times*, September 1992); "Travel-Related Cholera Cases Reported in U.S. Soar to All-Time High" (*Los Angeles Times*, September 1992); "Infectious Disease Threat Rising in the U.S." (*Los Angeles Times*, October, 1992; "The Private Pain of Prostatic Cancer: It is Killing More and More Older Men " (*Time* Magazine, 1992).

It seems that wherever you turn your attention, bleak messages about the health of humankind greet you. AIDS statistics appear so frequently in journals that we are becoming desensitized to the bad news: 1.5 million deaths projected in the U.S. by the year 2,000; one-third of the African population wiped out by the turn of the decade; AIDS rapidly becoming the number one health problem in Asia.

Adding insult to injury, more Americans lose access to a mediocre health-care system that already consumes 12% of the GNP (gross national product), adding more people to the already staggering 37 million with no health insurance at all. Advanced medical technology has made decent health care a rich man's privilege, too expensive for the working poor and even middle-class people.

The irony is that most of the money spent for health care goes to purposes other than the actual delivery of personal health care.  Physicians deal daily with the high costs of practicing medicine. They confront excessive administrative paperwork to satisfy requirements from insurance companies, in a largely futile effort to cut costs.  The present legal system has led to excessively high medical malpractice insurance premiums, and a defensive practice of medicine that by itself has added billions of dollars in costs. All these factors cost the physician and you, the patient, in health care dollars.

The price of prescription drugs has risen almost three times the consumer price index over the last nine years. Since more and more insurance companies cover only delivery of care, consumers are left to pay for their own medicines. It is not uncommon for retired people to pay $500 every month for medications.  And, adding fuel to the fire, many of the drugs that are being prescribed are advertised to doctors in misleading drug ads.  A UCLA study published in the June 1992 issue of the *Annals of Internal Medicine* found that not less than 60% of the pharmaceutical ads surveyed were in violation of federal regulations and warranted complete rejection or major revision.

And lastly, with cancer now striking one in three Americans and killing one in four, people like you and me have grown impatient and dissatisfied with therapies that don't work, cause severe side effects or make us feel like powerless non-participants in our own healing.  In my opinion, surgery, chemotherapy and radiation are effective only for small numbers of cancer victims and they have not significantly affected cancer rates: 600,000 people a year still die from this killer disease, and if anything, the rate has been climbing.

Americans are ready to replace toxic, expensive medications with safe, effective natural remedies and healing methods. I believe that doctors also are ready for these "new" medicines: too many doctors have lost their love for their profession, and not only because of increased government intervention. Partially too, they are more and more confronted with "incurable" difficult diseases, "mysterious" epidemics such as Chronic Fatigue and Immune Dysfunction Syndrome (CFIDS) for which modern medicine provides them very little in terms of prevention.

With a health care system that is bursting at the seams, it is no wonder that consumers are ready for something else. More and more patients have turned to such practices as homeopathy, herbology, acupuncture, and chiropractic. This has already been the case in Europe, where the British royal family are fervent enthusiasts of homeopathy; and in France, Belgium, Germany, Holland, and Spain, which offer many good homeopathic courses to physicians. Even in the U.S., there are signs that alternative healing practices and methods are being taken more seriously. The National Institutes of Health (NIH) responded to a congressional mandate to research alternative medicines. Unfortunately, only the relatively small sum of $2 million was set aside for the study. And much will depend on the set-up of the study: it must be designed by practitioners of the healing method that is under investigation. But I welcome the challenge if it is well done, mostly for the chance to show that these older, time-tested medicines will stand up to any scrutiny. The very fact that the government is willing to fund meditation, acupuncture, herbology and homeopathy opens up a whole range of possibilities in medicine.

Medicine must be responsible to the needs of <u>people</u> rather than to the needs of the <u>profession</u>. Organized medicine must take an honest look at itself, acknowledge that it does not have all the answers, and reach out to embrace other avenues to healing, as both orthodox and complementary medicine have much to offer. Each can fill in some of the gaps left by the other.

There are some encouraging signs that thinking is changing even in "traditional" medical circles. For instance, I was thrilled to see the new oath of Hippocrates, drawn up by the School of Medicine at Yale University.   It was administered for the first time in 1991. I think this beautiful oath says it all:

*"Now being admitted to the high calling of the physician, I solemnly pledge to consecrate my life to the care of the sick, the promotion of health and the service of humanity.*

*I will practice medicine with conscience and in truth. The health and dignity of my patients will be my first concern.   I will hold in confidence all that my patients relate to me.   I will not permit considerations of race, religion, nationality or social standing to influence my duty to care for those in need of my service.*

*I will respect the moral rights of patients to participate fully in the medical decisions that affect them. I will assist my patients to make choices that coincide with their own values and beliefs.*

*I will try to increase my own competence constantly and respect those who teach and those who broaden our knowledge by research.  I will try to prevent, as well as cure, disease."*

This oath clearly considers the wishes of the patient <u>and</u> the doctor: that we will assist our patients in making choices that coincide with their beliefs, and that a practitioner shall not be persecuted if he or she practices an alternative form of medicine.

The goal of this book is to give the power of healing back to the people.  Section One will teach you how to recognize good health, how to know who you are by using the ancient art of traditional Chinese medicine to recognize your weaknesses and strengths.  Knowing these will not only help you avoid disease, but even more, will put you on the right track to health -- by instructing you what foods you need, what triggering factors to avoid and what positive physical and mental steps you can take to reach health.

You have two choices: You can live in fear of impending diseases, which will only bring fear and despair to your heart (two emotions guaranteed to bring dis-ease and death at the end). Or, you can spend that same energy to look in the opposite direction -- the direction of health -- and take it to improve your health. Remember the famous words of the late President John F. Kennedy: "Ask not what your country can do for you, ask what you can do for your country." It is the same when it comes to health. *Don't ask what your body can do for you, ask yourself what you can do for your body!*

Section Two will explain the cause of any disease, even the most mysterious one. By recognizing the etiological factor behind your condition, you can put yourself back in control. In fact, this section will teach you how to go back into your past and construct a time line of events.

Section Three of the book is dedicated to homeopathy and the true domestic physician. It explains how homeopathy works, how to look for a good homeopath and how simple observations will give you the key to your personal health.

Section Four covers special topics like hypersensitive people (an ever-growing group of patients); CFIDS; alcohol and drug addictions; vaccination issues; the new threat of epidemic diseases; geriatric problems; and mercury intoxication. This section will teach you the secrets to these unsolved mysteries. A final chapter in this section will give you immediate help for acute situations. It includes a practical guide to self-help at home for such situations as delivery, post-operative care, sunburns and how to help your children get through their difficult growing up years without lasting damage.

When, with the help of this book, you have finally achieved balance in your life, it would be neglectful on my part not to teach you the methods to reach peak energy and strength in your life. That's what Section Five is all about. The result: the sky is the limit!!

This book will bring to you, the patient, the message that you are the employer of your health care provider. You are hiring a doctor for his or her services, and it is the doctor's duty to educate you so that you can take an active role in your own health. If you become a partner in your own health care as a result of this book, then my message has been successful. It is my hope that this book will give hope to millions of sufferers. May the encounter with new medicines put you on the road to a healthy, fulfilling life.

# SECTION ONE

## RECOGNIZE IMBALANCE
## IN YOUR BODY

# CHAPTER ONE

# WHAT IS GOOD HEALTH? DOES ANYONE KNOW?

Libraries and bookstores abound with books and magazines devoted to health and medical topics. After countless hours devoted to my own research in hundreds of books and journal articles, it has become clear to me that the emphasis in Western medicine is on <u>disease</u>, not health. Perhaps this is because most popular medical book authors are medical doctors or other professionals like chiropractors and Ph.D.s who feel obliged to put to good use their years of intense studying. The books, then, are merely a reflection of the type of medical education their authors have received.

**Set-Up for Miscommunication**

To get my M.D., I had seven years of medical training, receiving information about the most uncommon and rare diseases in medicine. Conditions that most doctors will probably never see in their careers are examined with a fine-tooth comb in medical school, making us physicians living encyclopedias (at least for some years). This practice gives recent graduates an omnipotent feeling and exuberant confidence when they leave medical school -- that not one germ in this world can hide from their competence.

Armed with all these facts about disease, a new resident is confident as he or she sits behind the desk that with one mighty stroke of the pen on the prescription pad the patient's health will be restored. It is a fairy tale notion of physician as magician:

amidst stars and lights, the patient feels refreshed and recharged. And then reality sets in: in walks the first patient. "Can I eat this? What do you think about fasting? Do you think colonic therapy would do me any good?" This is like lightning and thunderstorm to the young doctor, not the smooth, balmy weather he or she was promised. And things get worse. There are those patients who insist they are not well, and yet, all standard tests turn out to be normal. "You are healthy, my dear," the doctor says, because our infallible tests have said so. Never mind that the patient feels like hell the rest of the day. Never mind what the doctor was taught in medical school about clinical perception and etiology.

Here is where the doctor often fails. He or she is so over-whelmed with test results and information about <u>disease</u> that he or she loses sight of the signs of <u>health</u>. Not only do doctors not know the signs of health, they feel at a loss to restore them. This leads to irritability, misunderstanding, frustration and discontent-ment in patient and doctor alike. The end result is irreparable damage to the doctor-patient relationship. The patient may change doctors frequently, looking for something that the doctors have not been taught. The physician may become cynical and characterize such patients as "hypochondriacs." But the question remains: What are the hallmarks and signs of good health?

### The Nine Signs of Health

Attaining and maintaining perfect health is every person's dream. Hundreds of thousands of people have at some point in their lives launched a quest for this jackpot. But patients often tell me, "I have been behaving marvelously. I only eat the best organic foods, forego all pleasures in eating, and yet I still feel tired." If health were a static state which, once reached, you could keep forever, you would be on your way to the ultimate dream: living forever! However, this is far from true: you are not isolated in a plastic bubble, protected from all the elements in the world, so there are many modulating influences on your health: weather conditions, environmental factors, and above all, emotional factors and certain inherent predispositions to disease particular to your constitution. (For more on this, see Section Two.)

Just as nothing in life is absolutely black or white, so a <u>constant</u> state of perfect health is not sustainable. The best you can do is use all the forces of your mind and body to approach that ultimate health goal. Most of the time you may be zigzagging in your course toward your goal, sometimes grossly overshooting it, then overcorrecting it, but the bottom line is that you are always doing a balancing act. If you stop balancing, your health begins to decline. So the first step in becoming healthy is to stop thinking that you can ever let your guard down and rest on your laurels. Stop complaining that health is ever changing, and learn to accept that life is a challenge for all living beings. To help keep you dancing on the rope of life, here are nine signs that you can recognize as keys to successful health (Table 1).

---

**TABLE 1**

**ARE YOU HEALTHY: NINE SIGNS**
Do you want to know if you are healthy?
Check out these nine KEY SIGNS OF SUCCESSFUL HEALTH:

**Physical Signs:**

> REFRESHED SLEEP
> ADAPTABILITY
> APPETITE

**Psychological Signs:**

> CLARITY OF MIND
> SENSE OF WELL-BEING
> CALMNESS
> A SENSE OF HUMOR

**Spiritual Signs:**

> HUMILITY
> LOVE FOR LIFE ON EARTH

**Physical Signs**

### 1. Refreshed sleep

How many among you can say that you feel refreshed the moment you open your eyes in the morning? Are you smiling and ready to go as soon as you awaken? Or do you punch the alarm clock and wonder how you could feel this lousy when you just slept eight hours? There is a big debate as to how long you should sleep in order to feel well. Conventional wisdom holds that as you get older you need less sleep, or that when you suffer from a disorder such as CFIDS you should rest as much as possible, because any exercise is detrimental. But these rules of thumb refer to the quantity of sleep, not the quality. Yet, the latter is the only important parameter.

Are you subject to insomnia and restless sleep? Do you toss around in your bed, counting sheep or reading books, while the hours slowly tick away? Or do you fall asleep quickly only to awaken in the middle of the night, with your mind racing, clear as a bell, your body feeling as if it weighs a thousand pounds? Do you use the night hours to revise your whole day, sometimes your whole life? Or are you one of the very health conscious people who believe the statement that you have to drink at least eight glasses of water daily, even if you are not thirsty? (I know of no other living creature in this world who drinks when not thirsty except for homo sapiens.) Since you follow this unproven, harmful advice, you're likely to get up three times a night to go to the bathroom. And each time it is a struggle to fall back to sleep. Or maybe you are one of those oversensitive people who wakes up at the slightest noise or the slightest movement of your partner (who is snoring beside you as if even the detonation of an atomic bomb could not wake him or her up). Of course, I know many of you who love to go out to eat late at night, and need that extra glass of wine to calm you down for the night. Nevertheless, you may still be puzzled that you wake up around 1 a.m. or 2 a.m., while any acupuncturist could tell you that you are damaging your liver with your habits.

Refreshed sleep means also that you have taken no sleeping pills: I have yet to see the first sleeping pill that will give you this good, refreshed sleep. Maybe you are one of the big groups of people who wake up in a foul mood. No one can talk to you for the first hour, until you have gulped down three pots of coffee. You threaten to kill your kids or spouse if they say to you, "Isn't it a splendid morning?" (You ask yourself, doesn't that miserable husband or wife of mine understand that my eyes are not open yet and that my ears suffer from acute deafness?) Of course, there are those among you who have to work at night or have to nurse loved ones in their suffering, leading to a lack of sleep.

The reasons are many, but I can tell you that in my practice, 90% of my patients do not enjoy refreshed sleep. How can you expect to attain health if you are not charging your batteries at night, when the calming Yin energy replaces gradually the active Yang energy, calming down the spirit as well as the body? Refreshed sleep is one of the major signs of health.

### 2. Adaptability

The ability to adapt to different environments is also a major sign of physical health. The baby born without natural antibodies is perfectly well as long as it stays in its isolated bubble. But would you call that baby healthy? Bring it out in the normal world and it could be killed by its first infection. This might be an extreme form of incapability to adjust, but there are plenty of other examples, which are growing in numbers.

Environmentally sensitive people, also called universal reactors, experience often violent reactions to the slightest changes in environmental factors. On a trip to Australia, I was asked to visit a 42-year-old woman who could not attend my lectures because she was not able to leave her house. For 20 years she had been the victim of her illness that started two weeks after she was married. She was involved in a car accident, had multiple injuries and was hospitalized for six months. During her stay in the hospital, she received multiple courses of antibiotics (for infections that one can only catch in hospitals), and to the amazement of her doctors, she had not been able to leave her apartment ever since. In fact, she had to strip that apartment of any artificial materials. Only pure cotton materials could be there.

But although she was unable to leave this apartment for even five minutes, within the safety of the building, she looked radiant, healthy and would probably elicit the diagnosis of hypochondriac or hysterical patient. This unfortunate woman can hardly be called healthy, for she had lost one of the nine key signs of physical health: the ability to adjust to a normal world.

While this woman presents a dramatic picture (which unfortunately is not as rare anymore), countless millions of others are restricted in their adaptability to environment or diet. How many patients on a special limited diet cannot deviate one iota from the diet without getting sick? If that is all you can achieve, then you have not regained your health but you are artificially kept at a level of "comfort," not health. To be a healthy person capable of adaptability, you must be able to ingest one of those "bad" foods and not pay for it with decreased energy for the next following hours, or even days.

You should also be able to skip a meal and not become hypoglycemic. Weakness, trembling, headaches and cold sweats are symptoms experienced by the majority of people attempting to skip a meal or to fast. People in truly good health feel more invigorated and focused when they fast, not the opposite. Another example of maladjustment and bad health is people having a hard time adjusting to bad air quality like smog. A person with good adaptability will react temporarily with some sneezing, headache, sore throat or even pain in the chest, but the adaptive system is strong enough to rebound back to health. This safety device has to function at peak levels because daily assaults will happen at the most unexpected moments. This second sign of health is malfunctioning more and more in our population. The reason? I believe it is the unbelievable amount of stress factors, explained in Section Two, that relentlessly attack you. And the weaker among us are paying for it with our health.

### 3. Appetite

The first kind of appetite that comes to mind, of course, is the appetite for food. One of the first signs of discomfort is losing your appetite. The unfortunate thing is that sick people are often forced to eat, when fasting would be more appropriate. Have you ever watched sick animals? The first thing they do is stop eating. So stop forcing your sick child to eat and let the child consume what he or she desires.

A healthy appetite is an excellent indicator of vital strength. This is different from what some among you experience as easy satiety: you sit down at the table with a good appetite, yet after a few bites, you are full. This is definitely a sign of maldigestion and malabsoption. Or maybe you have the opposite experience -- even after eating huge amounts of foods, you are still not satisfied. There is a good possibility that, unbeknownst to you, parasites sit at your dining table.

Remember, a balanced appetite has nothing to do with those cravings that create hassle in your life. Some among you have "appetite" only for sweet things, pastries, fried foods, ice-cream or coffee. This kind of appetite is not included in this definition and most of the time is an obstacle to good health, rather than an indicator of it.

A different kind of appetite is the one for sex, equally important as the first when it comes to indicating good health. Sexual appetite seems to disappear even more quickly than the desire for food when you are sick. Besides the notorious headaches, other symptomatic discomforts will kill all desire for sex.

In the next chapter, Chapter Two on the Language of Disease, you will see that sexual libido is governed by a good functioning of your kidneys and liver. No small wonder that so many among you lose your libido, since numerous destructive acts are committed against these two organs. Overeating, ingesting drugs, alcohol and medications (sleeping pills, tranquilizers, anti-hypertensive medications), exposure to environmental toxic factors, too much water intake, exaggerated anger and frustration, sudden fears and anxieties, and hormonal disturbances are just some of those influences. However, this healthy sexual appetite has nothing to do with sexual excesses, in which too frequent masturbation and sexual intercourse will lead to a loss of fluids and disturbances in your health.

**Psychological Signs**

### 4. Clarity of mind

If you think it is the physical aspect of disease that drives people crazy -- think again! Because it is precisely the mind that seems to be playing games with you. You know you've lost it (your health) when: you can't remember the names of good friends; when you can't balance your checkbook, even if you only completed two transactions; when in the middle of a sentence you stop and ask your partner what you were trying to explain; when you start repeating yourself to the chagrin of your family because you simply forgot you gave all the details ten minutes ago; when you remember what day you got your first bicycle, but you forget what someone told you to get at the store five minutes ago. Sound familiar? You are not alone. This "brainfag," as we call it, is present in numerous chronic conditions, CFIDS being one of them. Most people who experience brainfag are too embarrassed and simply laugh at it, because it seems the only way to deal with it. You start blaming your age, menopause, your period, that last beer yesterday, but few among you realize it indicates that part of your health is gone.

Clarity of mind also means that your perceptions are accurate and realistic. How you perceive the world is most important. Tell most Americans that they have to skip a meal and they think they are going to die. In Somalia, people are dying from hunger but you don't see any riots, any killing between those starving humans. But there is a hurricane in Florida, and police have to intervene to curtail looting; people are ready to storm any place for food because they have been without food for one day. Makes you wonder who is civilized.

To attain better health, you have to change your perceptions about health and diet: you can't skip meals and exercise and hope that magic pills will do the job for you. With accurate perception, and the ability to keep things in proper perspective, your mind and emotions will not be in disarray.

### 5. A sense of well-being

It might be difficult to define this element of health, but anyone among you who has felt this way knows precisely what I mean. You might call it "sitting on the top of the world," "floating on cloud nine," or being "madly in love." You have the sensation that your feet are so light that they barely touch the ground. There is no weight on your shoulders, every step you take brings you closer to your goal than you thought, you have that irresistible feeling that nothing can go wrong. I don't think many Western physicians ask their patients whether they have felt this sense of well-being. They are far too much focused on lab test changes or results from administered therapies.

I remember a cancer patient who, after the usual radiation and operation, felt so miserable that she wanted some holistic support to lift her spirits as well as her energy. When she returned to visit the oncologist, he predicted doom and death because her CEIA test (blood test to indicate possible presence of cancer cells) had slightly increased. Never mind that the patient told him she felt better than she had felt in months. He didn't want to hear about it. This physician, whose highest ideal should be to support the patient and heal the soul as well as the body, had thoroughly upset this poor patient, who felt miserable for two days until her decrease of vital energy was restored by homeopathy.

We as physicians should never forget the "*power of the word.*" Hearing bad news is a shock to the system of the unprepared patient and will damage the immune system. On the other hand, medicine can never consider any therapeutic act -- be it an alternative or conservative method -- as successful if it is not able to create that sense of well-being in the patient. The first reaction of a patient to a correctly chosen homeopathic remedy is a sense of well-being even while the symptoms persist. When we observe this reaction in the patient, we know we are on our way to restoring health and that the remedy was a correct one. I would be remiss if I did not comment on the physical aspects of the sense of well-being. Freedom from pain in the physical body is a must for this important element of your health.

### 6. Calmness

To illustrate calmness, it may be helpful to picture the opposite: those who operate with extreme time-urgency or impatience in life. Have you ever been in the company of someone who drags you from one place to another, who never seems to have more than 1% of his muscles rested at the same time, who is tapping his feet, blinking his eyes, plays with that cigarette in his mouth and always seem to have too little time? The time never seems to go fast enough, the list of projects to do is only increasing. A person like this can drive you crazy. You are afraid to sit still for one minute in his company because he may accuse you of being lazy.

On the other hand, you might be better off to be in his company than in the company of one whose mind never seems to take a break. This kind of person seems to have high contempt for the slow minds of those around him, believing that he is the only one who really knows something. He is impatient with you, interrupts you in the middle of a sentence because he wants you to hear his opinion and then jumps from A to Z in his explanation because his racing mind skips every other letter in the alphabet. Of course, this brilliant mind wakes you up in the middle of the night because he just thought about this "cannot-go-wrong" phenomenal project. He does not need coffee, but it will be his favorite drink, since he always craves that next high. I don't know what you would do if you were married to a combination of both these types, but you would have my sympathy. While they are wrecking the health of everyone else around them, the time-urgent and impatient people really do the most damage to themselves. Predictably, this condition will burn them out, be it because of overstudy, lack of sleep or physical exhaustion. Human beings are not race cars. They need rest as well as activity. The Chinese paid much attention to what they called, "the freedom from passion on the emotional level." For them, there were no highs or lows, because in their infinite wisdom, they knew there was no Yang (high) without Yin (low). Every state of the mind was temporary, therefore there was no reason for them to be overly concerned or overly optimistic. This resulted in a dynamic and balanced state of serenity and calmness. A simpler lifestyle is a prerequisite to the attainment of calmness.

### 7. A sense of humor

"Laughter is the best medicine." Those were the immortal words of the late Norman Cousins. And if you think about it, your own common sense will agree. Have you ever met a person devoid of humor? His face looks like it was just soaked in vinegar, he will put forth in detail everything that is wrong in this world and will point out that everything is to be taken very seriously. For this type of person, laughter and humor inevitably are linked to debauchery and low lifestyle. He believes you should not let your guard down because doom is just around the corner. The Three Stooges films are a waste of time, and he would rather send the Marx brothers to another world. To this person, theater is only for people who have no imagination. How long can anyone stay with Mr. Pessimist? He drags you down in spirit and soul, sweeping over you like a tornado.

What a difference I have seen in patients who, in spite of severe health problems, always wanted me to tell them the latest joke and seemed to enjoy it when we, as a team, would not take their disease too seriously, but rather view it as an opportunity to see the humor and challenge of it. Often, it is this "sick" person who lifts your spirit, who makes your problems look like they are negligible and unimportant matters. You have so many facial muscles: let them work hard. It takes less muscle energy to smile than to frown. You would be surprised what it does for your health.

## Spiritual Signs

### 8. Humility

Humility is simply part of your health balance. *The simplicity of it is its beauty.* The antithesis of this quality is personified in Mr. Narcissist, somewhat related to Mr. Nux Vomica, whom you already met in the discussion about calmness. Mr. Narcissist does not take "no" for an answer, does not want to hear your opinion, and will dominate the conversation in any company (if anyone is willing to stick around). This person's ever-present of irritability and constant necessity to prove himself is destructive, according to Chinese medicine, to the liver. It is no coincidence that this character disorder is related to homeopathic liver remedies. These anger fits lead to gastrointestinal symptoms like stomach ulcers and constipation, to menstrual disturbances, to insomnia, headaches, even premature gray hair!

### 9. Love for life on earth

Having this quality means having an open heart to every living being on earth. If you are trying to improve your lifestyle, your diet, your personality, it will be fruitless unless you are willing to show charity. That means that you must love yourself first. How can you expect to contribute to the happiness of other people if you are in shambles yourself? You owe it to yourself to build up your own strength in order to share it with all life around you.

This unconditional love for all living beings does not come easily, but as long as you are without it, you will not have attained health. And I do mean all living beings. I am sometimes saddened to see how we mistreat animals in the same way as we mistreat human beings, all in the name of science. Do not forget plants, either, which can bring you so much joy. Neither forget the flowers which cheer you up when you are down. We owe a lot to plants and minerals. Wonderful homeopathic remedies have been derived from only 5% of what is present on earth. So much lies in nature, ready for us to explore, to bring relief to some of the most horrible diseases. We have to start respecting nature before it has lost all its secrets to our destructive actions.

### Four Pillars - the Foundation

Western medical science demands proof of validity from other healing methods. Acupuncture, homeopathy, and other healing methods are evaluated using the language and measurements of Western medicine. Let's turn the tables and see if Western medicine holds up to the standards of a complementary or holistic medicine, such as homeopathy.

Any form of medicine should adhere to *four strong pillars*. Without them, health will be like a temple supported by one column instead of four: the smallest wind, the slightest tremor will knock down your house of health. Would you keep building protection against wind or earthquakes, or would you try to build all four pillars and fortify them? Sounds like the most logical response, doesn't it? Let's look at what these four pillars are.

### 1. Neutralizing the Disorder

The first pillar is *neutralizing the disorder*. Does Western medicine accomplish this? Western medicine is a germ-oriented medicine. Whenever we don't know the cause of a disease, be it cancer, autoimmune disorders or CFIDS, we think that a virus or multiple viruses are the cause. Most medications are based on the principle, *"the contrary cures the contrary"*: if we have a germ, an anti-germ is the answer. If we have fever, an anti-fever remedy is indicated. If we have inflammation, numerous anti-inflammatory drugs are available. If you have pain, the doctor doesn't let you walk away without an "anti-pain" pill. It appears that modern medicine has this pillar strongly built.

In Western medicine, we are concerned with identification of the ever-changing, restless viruses and have to invent new weapons on a daily basis to combat them. This is a Herculean task under which mankind seems to crumble: tuberculosis (TB), gonorrhea, syphilis, AIDS, and CFIDS are gaining ground at a frightening rate. Western medicine, once heralded as the bastion and champion of the germ war, has lately suffered one defeat after another. Old forgotten epidemics seem to make a come-back, eating away at the once strong neutralizing pillar of Western medicine.

Homeopathy is no slouch when it comes to neutralizing germs. It is enough for the patient to see the calming effects of Belladonna or Aconite in sudden high fevers in children, to realize the enormous potential of homeopathic germ warfare. Of course the principle on which this is built is completely different.

Holistic medicine has a different viewpoint. It concerns itself less with the identification of the germ than with the "terrain" of the patient. As early as the 19th century, there was a saying: "The virus means nothing, the terrain is everything." No matter what viruses or bacteria are presented, homeopathy will be able to raise the vital energy of the patient, thus allowing his or her defenses to neutralize the disorder.

Holistic healing asks not who the invader is but how it could penetrate our defenses. What weakened us in the first place? Viruses, even the most fearsome, have been around for a long time, and coexist in our bodies from day one. Yet our susceptibility to viruses seems to have changed. The reason for this is explicitly explained in Section Two of this book, "The Causes of Disease."

Of course, there are some other major differences in neutralization of disease between Western medicine and homeopathy. Modern medicine often destroys much more than it ought to. I have yet to encounter a medicine without side-effects, many of which have to be counteracted with yet another medication. According to the World Health Organizations, iatrogenic diseases, or diseases caused as a result of a doctor's treatment, account for as much as one third of all illnesses. Just look around you and you know people who have been harmed by or are addicted to medications.

In the introduction I already touched on the exorbitant cost of medicine, which in itself can create enormous stress leading to disease. On the other hand, homeopathy, with its infinitesimal doses, is absolutely safe and very inexpensive. It truly follows the first rule of its master, Dr. Samuel Hahnemann, to bring "a gentle and rapid cure."

### 2. Restoring Health

Can Western medicine claim to accomplish this second pillar, to restore health? After reading carefully the nine signs of health discussed earlier, we would have to say that our traditional modern medicine fails miserably in this directive. Relief of a symptom or correction of a laboratory test result does not constitute restoration of health. A cure is a complete eradication of the <u>existence</u> of that problem. No wonder old epidemics are on the rise. "Modern" medicine, not knowing how else to give relief, has suppressed by drugs a single symptom from among many. A single one of the presenting symptoms no more represents the whole illness than one foot represents the whole man. There are times when this approach yields nothing, but inflicts much harm.

Hahnemann (the founder of modern homeopathy) in his wisdom said, "to restore health is to annihilate the whole, the entire disease, not just *suppress* certain symptoms." This discrimination is of primary importance. People usually call "cure" the disappearance of external manifestations of disease, such as constipation, skin rashes, vaginal discharge, etc. How often, as physicians, have we met those patients who demand treatment for certain unpleasant symptoms, due to an itch or minor discomfort? The patient has no idea what distinguishes *palliation* (symptomatic relief of symptoms) from a *genuine cure*. He has no idea, for instance, that a skin rash, an external symptom, is only one of the manifestations of a deeper affliction, often the least important one of the general trouble. And the physician in a hurry -- anxious to keep the patient as a client and through lack of understanding -- is too often tempted to take the easy but dangerous road of palliation, to suppress the external symptom. The physician, and of course the patient, do not recognize the cause and effect connection between suppression of superficial disturbances and the development of the related internal organ conditions.

All too often modern medicine relies on the science of pathology and laboratory tests. While they have their merit, there are dangers in this method of thinking. Often, pathology is a science practiced on the dead, not always useful to the living. I once heard a pathologist say, "We shall know how to cure this patient when we know the pathology." I then asked him: "When shall we know the pathology?" He replied: "When we have made a post-mortem." (In other words, when the patient is dead.) But while I feel that pathology is a strong point of Western medicine, laboratory tests are indicators that something very serious has already occurred.

When the laboratory tests can tell us what mankind hates and loves; when they can give us a complete image of man's rational mind with all its deviations from the norm; when they can tell which human beings are sensitive to cold, to heat or dryness; when they are able to furnish us with causes for the lack of resistance and susceptibility; when they reveal to us the real condition of inherited tendency -- then the laboratory will lead to a remedy for sickness. But unfortunately, laboratory tests cannot answer these questions, and in some cases, the tool has become the master!

It is discouraging to see how much physicians rely on test results to dictate a course of action with a patient. It is almost as if they forgot everything they were taught in medical school: the importance of clinical perception, etiology, lifestyle, etc. The thoroughly-rounded physician is one who adds to his knowledge of pathology and diagnosis the knowledge of a universal science like homeopathy.

### 3. Maintaining Health

Maintaining health can only be accomplished through education and lifestyle changes. Both should be within the purview of doctors who then could work in concert with their patients to accomplish this goal. But while public health courses exist in medical school, they mostly teach physicians how to look at statistics. Diet instructions, nutritional supplements, hygienic measures, are little -- if at all -- stressed, so that often inattention to them becomes a roadblock to the patient's recovery. Because of insufficient advice, acute diseases become chronic and stay chronic. Little do we realize that sometimes the chronic disease is a false one, just waiting for us to remove the maintaining cause, which can be as simple as an overdose of coffee intake.

### 4. Cultivating and Enhancing Health

Cultivating and enhancing health is another major roadblock. It is not enough to neutralize a virus. You have to compensate for the lost energy. Does an athlete after a long-time illness start running a marathon right away? After an illness, it is imperative to restore your lost vital energy. Neither drugs, nor medications, nor homeopathic remedies can do this. In Chapter 12 you will learn how to supplement that lost energy.

And so, after comparing Western medicine with alternative medicines on the strength of these four pillars, I conclude that Western medicine, because it is a disease-oriented science, only manages to satisfy stage one of the four pillars of health: it does neutralize the germs. But it fails to accomplish the other three objectives: restoring health, maintaining health and cultivating and enhancing health. Alternative medicine is health-oriented and is built equally strong on all four pillars.

TEMPLE OF HEALTH
BUILT ON THE FOUR PILLARS

# CHAPTER TWO

## DO YOU REALLY KNOW WHO YOU ARE? THE LANGUAGE OF DISEASE

The language of disease, like any other language, must be learned. For thousands of years, medicine has been trying to understand disease by its own methods, taking little note of the language in which disease expresses itself. When your vital force is distressed, it communicates through external signs, or objective symptoms, and the so-called subjective symptoms, which must be obtained from the patient. Chinese medicine was far advanced in diagnostics: thousands of years of observation led to a system of such accuracy that even modern techniques have not been able to duplicate it. Their techniques allow the physician to know much about the patient before even one question is asked.

### Understanding the Patient

As James Tyler Kent the famous homeopath said, "The study of the face is a delightful study and a very profitable one." When patients present themselves to practitioners of alternative medicine, the practitioners learn much from their facial expressions, manner, mode of action, habits, dress, and all other external manifestations. Is the patient well-kept, his hair combed meticulously, with an anxious look on his face? Or does he present himself with a slouchy gait, with dirty clothes, unshaven, and irritable? A man shows his business of life in his face; he shows his method of thinking, his hatreds, his longings and his loves. For instance, how easy it is to pick out a man who has never loved to do anything but eat. Some faces manifest the hatred of a life they have been forced to live. Much is learned from this first well-observed picture of the patient that will guide the wise physician. The science of homeopathy adds a special human artistry: the perception of who the human being to be healed really is and the recognition of his (or her) unique makeup.

Other objective signs such as the tongue picture and pulse reading will unlock the mystery of the patient even further. And yet, during the course of such an examination, not one question has been asked! Even in asking about the symptoms, the alternative doctor's questionnaire is totally different from that of the orthodox doctor. Not one symptom can be too peculiar or strange for the homeopathic physician or acupuncturist. On the contrary, often a seemingly odd symptom will be the key for his prescription. Yet the same strange symptom will be brushed aside by the Western physician as something either unimportant or incomprehensible.

In this chapter, you will learn how to recognize the different prototypes of people. When you do so, the past, present and future will unfold to you! Understanding these prototypes will teach you why you get certain maladies, why you are not feeling well today, and where you are headed if you can't get yourself in balance. To know which type you are is an invaluable guide to maintaining or restoring your health. It will give you a fun and useful tool, to see who it is that you really married, who your friends really are and even why you chose them. If nothing else, it will be a comfort to you to know why you are acting strange one day and happy the next. While most of you will recognize yourself in one particular type, sometimes you will find yourself in two or more different types. There is nothing wrong with being like this. In fact, possessing some elements of the different types can be a strength.

Five thousand years ago, the Chinese classified people in five different classes: the *earth* type, the *wind* or wood type, the *metal* type, the *fire* type and the *water* type. Each of these types can present itself as a healthy picture or a sick picture. Often these pictures will be the opposite of each other. In the following descriptions, I have highlighted the <u>negative results</u> of each organ's imbalance, in an effort to help you realize that an imbalance does indeed exist. From this point, we will proceed to the causes and cures. Let's start our journey through the maze of human nature to discover which type best describes you.

## The Five Chinese Classifications

### The Earth Type

The earth type is governed by the energy of the spleen, pancreas and stomach. Physically you are more the gregarious type. You always fight with your weight, and water retention and cellulitis are no strangers to you. Sometimes you may forego your meals for a piece of fruit or a sweet. In fact, these cravings can become an obsession, and a meal without dessert is unheard of. It is therefore not uncommon that you are suffering from hypoglycemic attacks: you are not able to skip a meal without experiencing faintness, clammy sweats, headaches and irritability. You feel that you need a piece of sugar to get your energy up in the middle of the afternoon but, alas, too often, you crash after feeling the limited high of your sweet intake. This begins a vicious cycle, necessitating the intake of yet another sugar booster. You are the one who, at age 60, all of a sudden shows signs of adult onset diabetes. Besides sugar, you like beef and rice. You hate exercise and look flabby and obese, in a body that has lost its muscle tone. You often start sweating with the slightest exertion, and going upstairs scares you to death since you just barely make it.

You have grown outwards rather than upwards, look pasty and white with cold, clammy hands and feet. You have a general sensation of being cold as if your feet were wrapped in wet stockings. Humidity or dampness is your enemy. Damp, overcast days will dampen your mood and make you feel more sluggish. On those days you will go to bed with your socks on. As if this is not bad enough, you will wake up at night with cramps in your feet and legs. You have a tendency to be constipated, or perhaps you alternate between constipation and diarrhea. Due to your constitution, you are easily bloated because of quick fermentation  giving way to abdominal discomfort and frequent belching.

As strong as you might look, you have tendencies to catch colds with a lot of mucus formation.  You drool on your pillow and your dentist notes the presence of canker sores in your mouth.  Then there is a tendency to recurrent attacks of cold sores on your lips (herpes simplex I), redness and soreness of the eyelids, bleeding and receding gums. In fact all the mucosa in your body seem to be sensitive; you have anal itching and your bladder can be irritated.  You bruise easily -- you are often astonished at the size of bruises you have without running into something.  Your nose bleeds easily. You feel dizzy when you stand up after having been in a horizontal position.  You usually look pale but sometimes you have this false plethoric appearance: you blush or flush easily, giving you a momentary and falsely healthy appearance.  Your tongue looks white or yellow. This coating is especially visible in the middle but sometimes the whole tongue can be covered with a white coating.  Sometimes your lips are dry and thin with no sense of taste.  Your urine looks deep yellow. You love perfumes because you have an excellent sense of smell.

When you feel good, you are well-organized and very methodical.  In fact you are a very analytical, intelligent and obsessive-compulsive person.  You are a compulsive list writer and you can't function unless you have written down everything very carefully on little scraps of paper.  On the block, you are known as the mother/father type.  You are always ready to listen to everyone's problems, often to the extent that you are exhausted.  This is because you are a sympathetic listener and you feel responsible for everything that happens around you.  In fact you can't stand to see the bad news on TV or to read about it in newspapers.  You turn the TV off with a sense of inner torment, as if you had taken the suffering of the world on your shoulders.

Being this "super mom" type does not always pay off.  You can take so much on from others that you can collapse from overwork. You feel overwhelmed and worried, especially about things in the past.  At that point you become listless, start overeating, feel apathetic and lazy.  In those moments, the slightest effort makes you both intellectually and physically tired. You start becoming easily discouraged and depressed and are often afraid of many things. You become an insomniac because of lack of motivation and feeling useless. You are not very tidy, but you know where everything is. You desire order in your own world and you are obsessed with your bookshelves. Your desk seems to be a mess, yet nobody can touch it because you know exactly where to find everything. You love singing, music and dancing if you find the energy.

Governed by the spleen, pancreas and stomach, there are a myriad of conditions and diseases to which you are prone: gout; pre-diabetes and diabetes; hypertension; dizziness; stroke; arthritis; osteoporosis; urinary stone formation; digestive disorders; hiccoughs; edema; prolapse of the uterus, rectum or bladder; bleeding disorders and excess bleeding with menses; hemorrhoids; and immuno-suppressed conditions such as candidiasis, cancer, leukemia, and AIDS.

### The Metal Type

The metal type is governed by the energy of the lungs and large intestines. You are more of a longitudinal type with a small head, narrow shoulders and minute feet. You are slender with a tendency to stoop. Your face color is predominantly white and grayish. When ill you tend to look sickly and your features are drawn. You are very sensitive to catching cold, especially with laryngitis. Your voice seems to be the weakest spot of your defense system. Whenever you have a flu, it is a flu that drains you completely -- you feel a weariness, general weakness, sleepiness and a generally dopey feeling. At that moment, there is great aversion to the least effort.

You seem to improve when you sweat and are exposed to fresh air. However, you don't much like exercise because you can easily become out of breath. Congestion, particularly in the head, and hoarseness are often part of your symptoms. You suffer from congestive, throbbing headaches, aggravated by noise and motion. You love spicy, pungent foods rather than sweets. But chocolate and ice cold drinks are also high on your list, because your mouth is almost always dry. You love to take a nap and in fact, a 15 minute nap refreshes you.

Most of your physical problems relate to the skin: there are dry, flaky, unhealthy looking rashes, aggravated during the winter and in dry climates. You seem to be plagued by obstinate constipation. You have no urge to defecate and even soft stools are passed with great difficulty. Your skin can be dry and wrinkled. Itching will get worse while in a warm bed and with a hot shower. You suffer from night sweats and low-grade fevers throughout the day. The soles of your feet and the palms of your hands are warm. You either have sparse or superfluous hair growth on the body, but not the head. Although you can be cold-sensitive, dryness is your main enemy. Changes on the tongue (redness or a fur) are seen on the anterior third.

Psychologically, you suffer a great deal of anguish and worry about the future. You experience grief, and weep easily. You also suffer from claustrophobia and have a fear of crowds. There can be great sadness and pessimism in you, making it difficult for other people to live with you. On the bright side, you are simple, accurate, even clairvoyant at times. Your sense of justice makes you an excellent judge. You are hypersensitive to light, smells and noises. Other fears include fear of storms, solitude, diseases and death. You are rather sentimental and are interested in other people, although you have a tendency to withdraw because of your natural shyness. You love to be consoled when you are sad. Because your energy is available in spurts, you are only able to be productive in stops and starts. Enthusiasm easily changes to feelings of disgust, making your pace of life irregular. This alternation between excitement and depression makes you seem rather unstable, but it is just that you are subject to a changeable energy level.

As a metal type, there are various diseases to which you are prone, including: lung diseases like asthma, emphysema, recurrent flus, colds, and laryngitis; dry, painful throat and chronic coughs; depression and anxiety; edema and water retention; constipation; nasal problems (bleeding, dryness with crust formation, polyposis); eczema and other skin rashes.

### The Water Type

The water type is defined by the energy of the kidneys and bladder. If you fall into this category, you have a large head, narrow shoulders and a large abdomen. You like movement because standing still for any length of time makes you very tired and brings on those lower back pains to which you are prone. You have an immense fear of cold because, of all the personality types, you are by far the most chilly person. In fact, your whole body -- or certain parts, especially your hands and feet -- feel icy cold. You are prone to watery stools and your urine will be clear like water. You have a tendency towards brittle head hair which falls out easily. You are generally fleshy and appear healthy, but you suffer easily from rheumatism and other joint disorders. You may get stiffness and pains in the lumbar region and your hands can be swollen and stiff first thing in the morning. Your general stiffness and pain disappear after moving around, but the symptoms return in the evening because of exhaustion.

Depending on whether you are male or female, you may have problems with diminished libido, impotence or frigidity. There is often a total lack of sexual appetite, with indifference towards your partner. Sometimes you may care less if you ever had sexual intercourse again. You only have sex out of obligation and, if you are a woman, may fake orgasms. You tend to have black circles under your eyes in the morning and you look like you did not get any sleep. You crave salty things and ice cold water, even with ice cubes. If you are a man, you can suffer from nocturnal emissions and night sweats, leading to a loss of vital energy. Your dreams are frequently nightmares leading to unrefreshed sleep. You are disturbed by heart palpitations. Women who are water types suffer from a vast array of menstrual irregularities: either no menstrual period at all, but more often scanty flow or increased frequency of periods. Your knees feel weak, there is often dental bone loss with a tendency to osteoporosis elsewhere in your body. At night, you get up frequently to urinate.

Psychologically, you are the personality type who has the most phobias. Not one phobia is foreign to you. You experience agoraphobia (fear of open places), fear of flying, heights, the dark, being alone, being in crowds, public speaking, being in enclosed spaces, fear of animals, the dentist, bridges, and above all, fear of losing control. In fact, you predict gloom and doom everywhere. You experience anticipatory anxiety leading to diarrhea and upset stomach. You dread going to a public place or to the theater for fear of having diarrhea. You are always wondering: "What if..?" There is an intense fear of contamination. You would rather avoid shaking hands or kissing out of the fear of catching a disease. You avoid public toilets for the same reason. You can be very indecisive and yet you can become very hasty and impulsive. You want to get things over before they are finished. You are constantly excited, in a hurry, and worried, with trembling all over your body.

Diseases to which you are prone include: hypertension, insomnia, convulsions, epilepsy, rheumatic disorders, back pains, anxiety and phobias. Also, hair loss on the head, ear problems (deafness, tinnitus), nervous diarrhea, recto-colitis, asthma, irregular heartbeat, impotence, frigidity, edema, kidney stones, adrenal exhaustion, vertigo, and urinary incontinence.

### The Wood or Wind Type

The wood/wind type describes the energy of the liver and gallbladder. You are rather tall, with large shoulders, small hands and feet, and a long, thin nose, which can often be swollen and red. You have tight muscles and tendons. Your weak points of the body, besides the muscles, are your eyes and nails. When you are out of balance you can have fingernails that are brittle, dry and flaky with ridges; black floaters in the eyes; blurred vision and night blindness; and irritation of the eyes, including acrid tearing or dry eyes. The eyes are alive and intelligent looking, sometimes contrasting with the physically run-down appearance. Your eye and nail symptoms are directly related to a malfunctioning of your liver. Don't forget that this organ is **the** detoxification factory for your body. When the liver becomes overwhelmed with toxins, it will show its malfunction (aside from constipation) first in the eyes. Amenorrhea or the absence of menstrual periods (the Chinese called it "dried up blood in the liver"), can be common. The face can be yellowish and prematurely wrinkled, making you appear older than you really are. The hair is prematurely gray. Males among you can suffer from impotence: although desire can be present, you have difficulty achieving an erection.

You love hot drinks, warm foods and sweets but your favorites are chocolate and sour foods. You have an inability to digest fat foods which will often lead to distension and gas. Therefore, you can't stand to have tight clothes around the waist; even burping and passing wind will bring you no relief. You don't like onions and beans because of the gas they cause. You love the fresh air and hate warm stuffy rooms. You will be the first one to throw the windows open, even when you are chilly. Often, you complain about easy satiety: because you ferment quickly and bloat, after a few bites you can feel full. You feel that you have to eat frequent small meals, because you are the first one to suffer from hypoglycemia. Often, you have a bitter or metallic taste in the mouth.

In the morning, you are grouchy and don't want to talk to anyone, because most of the time you have not had refreshed sleep. Often, you experience leg cramps, spasms and stiffness of the joints during the night. Bloating is especially visible below the navel. Sometimes you feel pain in your right shoulder or pain radiating to the lower corner of the right shoulder-blade. Your lowest point of energy during the day will be between 4 a.m. and 8 p.m. You often wake up between 1 a.m. and 3 a.m. You feel better when you keep on moving around. You don't like to lie down on your right side because of the feeling of tension and fullness you feel in the liver area. You are very sensitive to wind and can suffer from many allergies. Those women among you that gain or lose several pounds during the course of a single day, or who gain more than the usual amount of weight premenstrually, usually have a dysfunction of the liver. Disturbances of your liver energy can be seen on the sides of the tongue: it can be swollen, bluish-purplish, with indentations of the teeth imprinted in the tongue.

Psychologically, you can be quite a character. If you are in balance you excel in your judgment and decision-making, which makes you the perfect executive or general in the army. However, you are often ruled by your hot temper. You can be irritable, angry and easily frustrated. Your liver excess will make you shout, which you like to do at moments when you feel like an erupting volcano. On the other hand you can be melancholic and repress your feelings, which damages the harmonizing function of the liver. If you are a woman, you have the worst form of PMS: you want to be left alone because you know you are impossible to live with around that time of month. You can be depressed and out of control with outbursts of anger.

You are mostly intelligent with a sharp, quick wit, but you can be very authoritative and cannot bear being contradicted. Your ego can be bloated and you often compare yourself to others. Underneath your domineering appearance there is really deep, hidden anxiety and a lack of self-confidence. You have a low self-esteem with fear of performance (also of sexual performance, especially for men), fear of new situations and new commitments. You can be haughty and dictatorial. Often, in a later stage, because physical symptoms will affect your mind, intellectual efforts can become tiring and the desire to be active and hard-working can disappear. In the end you will feel run-down physically and mentally.

The diseases which you are prone to have a lot to do with your unbalanced emotions. These include: stomach ulcers, hypertension, insomnia, bloating, gas and constipation, nausea and vomiting, menstrual irregularities (amenorrhea or excessive bleeding), hayfever and other allergies, migraines, muscle cramps, muscle spasms in both small muscle (eyelid twitching) and large muscle groups, nail conditions, eye disturbances, hepatitis, jaundice, and stroke.

### The Fire Type

The fire type involves the energy of the heart and pericardium. It should be noted here that in Chinese medicine, the pericardium has a double function: it is resonsible for the circulation and also the sexual function of the human being. The heart is the supreme master of the organs, and it is also the residence of the spirit.

If you are a fire type, you have a red face, small head, pointed chin, round back, shoulders and hips. You have small hands and feet. Since the heart controls the blood, the majority of the symptoms of menopause (hot flushes, palpitations and nervousness) are heart symptoms. You are nervous, easily excitable and want to move around all the time. You are longitudinal, slender and well toned. You are prone to sudden onset of headaches, palpitations, and blushing. You are the sportive type for whom time never goes fast enough. The weak point in your body is the tongue. Disturbances of heart energy are often seen on the tip of your tongue: it becomes dry and red. The tongue can be painful and dry with canker sores, and there can be a bitter taste in the mouth. Lips and nails can have a bluish color. The face can look reddish. You may experience dizziness, nose bleeds, and insomnia. Inflammation of the tongue and stomach (glossitis and stomatitis), and an oppressive feeling in the thorax are all possible.

Psychologically, you are the enthusiastic type. You are passionate and warm with a bouncing personality and powerful emotions. You laugh easily, sometimes hysterically, even at your own follies. You excel in insight and understanding. You are very impulsive with periods of uncontrolled joy or sadness. You are a compulsive talker and laugher, and at parties you are the center of attention. You are very social and love to meet people, love to travel, dance and play music. You sweat easily during exercise. You can have fear of cold. In extreme cases, you can become manic-depressive, with sudden mood swings. This condition may include muttering to yourself, delirium and, ultimately, coma.

You are prone to stroke, hypertension, hysteria, insomnia, circulatory disturbances (Raynaud's disease), delirium, agitation, dry cough, heart diseases, aphony (inability to speak), discomfort with menopause (including hot flashes, palpatations and nervousness), diseases of the tongue, and fright.

Most of you will recognize yourselves in one or more type. The negative aspects of these organs have been described in order to help you to recognize which organ is in imbalance. It should guide you to react with common sense. The other chapters in this book will direct you -- once you recognize imbalance in your body -- to look for triggering factors and proper counter measures to take.    May this chapter be the beginning of the desire to understand yourself better and therefore, to take a more active part in the maintenance of your health.

# CHAPTER THREE

## CONSTITUTIONAL TYPES: KNOW YOUR CHILDREN!

*"No knowledge is perfect unless it includes an understanding of the origin -- that is, the beginning; and as all man's diseases originate in this constitution, it is necessary that this condition should be known if we wish to know his diseases."*

*--Paracelsus (1493-1541)*

*Constitution* is the aggregate of the physical and vital powers of an individual, or, put another way, his or her qualities, temperament or disposition. Constitution is both racial and hereditary. Under the influence of heredity, it is an ensemble of invariable functional characteristics manifested by the individual during the whole course of his or her life. Some homeopaths claim that it was Constantine Hering, M.D. who is responsible for this notion, while others cite James Tyler Kent, M.D. as its source. But for any homeopath who has read the 6th edition of the <u>Organon</u>, written in 1842, there is no doubt. Dr. Samuel Hahnemann, the author of that bible of homeopathy, clearly states in Paragraph 5:

*"Useful to the physician in assisting him to cure are the particulars of the most probably exciting cause of the acute disease, as also the most significant points in the whole history of the chronic disease, to enable him to discover its fundamental cause, which is generally due to a chronic miasm. In these investigations, the ascertainable <u>physical constitution</u> of the patient (especially when the disease is chronic), his moral and intellectual character, his occupation, mode of living and*

*habits, his social and domestic relations, his age, sexual function, etc., are to be taken into consideration."*

In plain modern language, this paragraph means that when the homeopathic physician takes the case of a chronically ill person, he has to take into account the causes of the disease, the constitution of the patient, as well as his lifestyle. Homeopathy is primarily concerned not with the object, i.e., the diagnosis of the disease, but with the *subject* (the patient), and with the principle of <u>individualization</u> which can be achieved therapeutically only by homeopathy. An example will clarify this. There are three abstract terms forming the essential object of disease:

> • **The causes**
> • **The subject**
> • **The effect**

Traditional Western medical science, chiefly analytical in its method, is focused on the search for the causes. For instance, if a patient has a sore throat, the main object is to find out the pathological causal agent, the specific microorganism responsible. When the etiology (cause) is determined, the patient is treated accordingly. However, Western medicine neglects the variations of the effects of a given cause on different people. Why is it that one person attacked by a flu bug will be lying in bed, completely exhausted, with sleepiness and weariness, whereas someone else exposed to the same virus will exhibit only a subtle cough? Modern medicine has ignored the constitution, the occupation, mode of living, moral character, social and domestic relations of its patients. This is a serious handicap for the physician. For instance, given two cases of pneumonia due to the same agent, both patients can have the same lab and x-ray results. But one may be stuporous, drowsy, weary and depressed while the other is delirious, anxious, restless and sleepless. For the homeopathic practitioner, this means two different remedies with different prognoses; for the Western-trained doctor, it is the same treatment plan.

## Only Dormant Symptoms Can Appear

Why did those two patients with pneumonia show such different symptom complexes?  Why is it that patients may react differently to the same medications, the same pathological agent (virus, bacteria, yeast), or to the same physical or emotional trauma?  Have you not seen for yourself how one person reacts to a grief situation with despondency, suicidal tendencies and total withdrawal, whereas someone else reacts to the same situation with a renewed vigor to go on with life, to be invigorated by the challenge?   Is it not strange that one patient demonstrates horrible side-effects from a certain medication, whereas another patient might show minimum reaction, or none at all, to the same therapeutic agent?

The same picture shows up in the proving of homeopathic remedies.  Different people who were taking the same doses of the same homeopathic agent displayed different symptoms. Only a limited number of the known symptoms of that remedy would show in each individual prover. (A prover is a healthy person who will test the remedy on himself.) Whenever I prescribe a homeopathic remedy for one of my patients, I let them read the clinical picture of their remedy in my Materia Medica.  Some say: "I have a lot of symptoms from this remedy picture, but I don't have such and such symptom as here described."

The only explanation for this is that any patient or prover will exhibit only those symptoms that ***already lie dormant within him***. When Hahnemann proved the first remedies on himself (Cinchona or Peruvian bark) he stated : "All the symptoms that *I* usually experienced with intermittent fever made their appearance." It would be ridiculous to believe that this Peruvian bark would cause the same reaction in every single person on earth.  Symptoms may be aroused in a constitution through the influence of disease, but only those symptoms that already are dormant within, be it as a residue from an earlier illness or the beginning of a new one, are the ones that will appear. This should be a warning to homeopathic prescribers who think that some symptoms are   essential or obligatory before you can prescribe a certain remedy.  There is no ideal drug picture out there. Patients have to realize that if they read about Pulsatilla that the Pulsatilla perfectly matched to them is non-existent in this world. It is the "similar" that we look for, not the "same" nor the exact. The prefix "Homeo" in homeopathy means *similar, not same.*

## Purpose of Constitutional Remedy

Certain homeopathic prescribers believe that a constitutional remedy is waiting to be unearthed in every chronically ill person. These physicians believe that finding this ultimate gem will effect a miraculous cure. Many times, the constitutional remedy <u>*will*</u> strengthen the patient or annihilate the patient's susceptibility to a certain disease. A certain constitutional picture is helpful in diagnosing an imbalance, and can be a source of pleasure to the patient confronted with a difficult and long-lasting illness, as well as the practitioner. Even Hahnemann in his time (around 1800) found that *acute* illnesses, sporadic fevers, epidemic illnesses and venereal diseases (gonorrhea and syphilis) were radically healed by homeopathic remedies.

But the healing of chronic maladies alluded him until near the end of his life, when he formulated the answer to this problem in his theory of "miasms." A *miasm* is the predisposition which makes the disease possible. It is a certain constitutional state upon which certain diseases may readily implant themselves. (See Chapter Five for more on the theory of miasms.) Practitioners of Western medicine, however, still dread treating chronic illnesses and are now exactly at the beginning, frustrating stage that Hahnemann was around the year 1810.

What would happen to those chronically ill patients, now and then? Through acute homeopathic remedies, or today's modern medications, the patient would sufficiently recover to believe himself in pretty good health, and even cured. This state could last for several years, but sooner or later, because of gross dietary mistakes, climate factors, emotional factors or an injury, one or more of the former symptoms would reappear. The relapse would be accompanied by new symptoms, which would be more resistant to treatment. New prescriptions would follow, but each time new symptoms would crop up, they would be treated inadequately and imperfectly or some not at all! Some improvement in lifestyle, if recommended by the physician, might bring about a "remarkable" remission, during which time the physician might deceive himself that the patient had recovered. But the end result is always the same: the progress of the disease was a little delayed, but it was never cured. The beginning of the treatment was spectacular and promising, the continuation unfavorable, the ultimate progress hopeless. While Hahnemann only had to deal with the progress of the disease itself, modern physicians find themselves troubled by the double symptom complex of the disease and the iatrogenic (medication- or treatment-induced) symptoms.

This just illustrates how we *suppress* many symptoms and fool ourselves into thinking that we have brought about a cure. What the body wisely either tries to bring to the surface to get our attention (the rashes) or tries to limit to a part of the organ, our treatments push back into the body, with often catastrophic results. You see numerous examples in the treatment of skin diseases where we put creams on rashes to push the disorder inwards and create much more serious diseases. I have seen in my practice countless patients treated with chemotherapy or radiation come back with their cancer having spread to other parts of their bodies. If a treatment does not increase most of our Nine Signs of Health, it should be banished and research money should go to support the medicines that will increase those signs.

It is in these cases that a constitutional remedy, after treating the acute stage with a different remedy, will increase the vital force of the person. Only then can we really stop progress of disease, because we have restored health, not suppressed symptoms. By the same token, patients should refrain from pressuring their physicians into overtreatment of cosmetic, innocent local diseases like rashes, warts, or scars. The only good treatment is to help bring those local disorders to the outside, not push them inward. Only homeopathy and medicines aimed at restoring the vital energy can do this.

## The Five Constitutional Groups

Classifying people into different constitutional types has been done since ancient times, and undoubtedly, new theories will be found in the future. The Chinese 5,000 years ago had their five types as described in Chapter Two (water, fire, etc). Hippocrates listed four types: bilious, nervous, sanguine and lymphatic type. The German homeopath Grauvogl, whose *Textbook of Homeopathy* was published in 1865, described his three types as Oxygenoids, Hydrogenoids and Carbonitrogens.

I will use a combination of Chinese methods and others to describe the different homeopathic children's constitutions under these five temperaments:

> - **the Digestive type**
> - **the Moist, Cold Phlegmatic type**
> - **the Nervous, Air type**
> - **the Choleric type**
> - **the Sanguine type**

Most of the time, the descriptions apply to both sexes. Sometimes, as in Pulsatilla, I mention "she" more than "he," since the character type is observed more in the female sex. But don't let this fool you: we also have male Pulsatillas and female Nux Vomicas.

This chapter is intended for parents to understand their children, as well as for adults to understand their own roots of disorders and to be able to understand their basic natures.

### The Digestive Type

There are three important constitutional remedy types falling under this category: the Calcarea Carbonica, the Baryta Carbonica and the Silicea Type.

**1. *The Calcarea Carbonica Child (Calc. Carb.)***

Many U.S. children are born Calcarea Carbonica types. This is the baby born with a huge abdomen, fat and fleshy. The blue eyes stand out in the large head with a pale face, sickly looks and listlessness. Everything about the baby looks flabby, with lax muscles and weak bones. The bloated abdomen is created by severe constipation. The baby or adolescent has large stools only every three days, but surprisingly, this seems to give him no discomfort. As he grows up, it is evident that there is a delayed, slow development: the fontanelles stay wide open, the teeth appear late, he is slow to walk and he seems to sweat profusely from his head and scalp, even when he is not exerting himself. The hands and feet are usually cold and the Calc. Carb. child always feels chilly. He suffers from recurrent colds and ear infections, and eczema or diaper rash is often seen in the newborn. Often he suffers from infected glands. He loathes physical effort, because any muscular and even intellectual effort makes him feel worse. He gets out of breath easily when going up stairs. He craves undigestible foods (dirt, chalk, plaster, etc.), ice cream and soft-boiled eggs, but loathes milk because it gives him gas and distension.

This is the good-natured kid, the one who always shares with his peers. He is highly sensitive to everything he sees on TV and hears from others. Often, he will cry about something horrible he sees on TV. He is the child that asks you a million questions about God and his existence. As he grows up, this sensitivity, as well as his chilliness, persists. He loves to go to bed with his socks on and needs the electric blanket, even though it leads to increased perspiration at night.

Calc. Carb. children are worriers and often feel overwhelmed by their sense of responsibility: they want to do their homework, but also feel very responsible to help at home or take care of younger siblings. No wonder they sometimes get overwhelmed and collapse from overwork. They might stay Calc. Carb. people all their lives and become these super moms and dads with an obsession for writing lists about everything they need to do that day. Often, a good percentage of these Calc. Carb. children will evolve around the time of puberty into the **CALCAREA PHOSPHORICA** (Calc. Phos.) type. They have suddenly grown into these longilineal, (tall and thin) children. While the Calc. Carb. child has a tendency to grow into short, stocky individuals, the Calc. Phos. type grows up, rather than outwards. They become slim and have good figures, but remain chilly. They become more lively, more irritable and easily excited. However, they remain easily fatigued physically and mentally. Calc. Carb. children might have delayed puberty: it is as if they want to stay in this delayed tendency of growth.

As the child grows up, he may remain either Calc. Carb. or Calc. Phos., but he can evolve into a Silicea or Natrum Muriaticum type, or in case of Calc. Phos., to a Phosporus type. These types are described later in this chapter.

### 2. *The Baryta Carbonica Child (Bar. Carb.)*

The Baryta Carbonica child is a more unfortunate child than Calcarea Carbonica. He is an exaggerated version of the latter with delayed physical and mental development. Bar. Carb. children usually look sickly, emaciated and old. Their tonsils are big, they are sensitive to cold and they are susceptible to colds. They are late in walking and talking because of psychic retardation, and they do not care to play. They are clumsy, inattentive, and hide behind their mothers' skirts because they are afraid of strangers. The lack of intellect can range from low IQ to total retardation. They are unable to make decisions. They are aggravated by the slightest exposure to cold and dampness. Growing up, they have a precocious puberty.

### 3. *The Silicea Child*

These children are the typically Nordic types. They look like little angels, with bright, shiny eyes, fine hair and blue eyes and are neat as dolls. They are excessively clean and orderly, quite a contrast to the previous types. Like Calc. Carb. children, they also have big square heads with a late closing of the fontanelles. Their nails are brittle and their hair falls out easily. Their big heads and abdomens contrast with their thin legs. They lack stamina and are stooped. They are slow in learning how to walk. They hate wind and so like to cover their heads with a hat.

They look very delicate, are very cold sensitive and have sweaty feet. They can't stand to get their feet wet or cold. They are very picky in their eating habits although they might crave eating sand. They also like salt and usually are very thirsty. Their skin is pale and even the slightest wound has a tendency to get infected. These children often suffer from recurrent ear infections and skin infections, and have chronic headaches beginning at the nape of the neck and radiating above the right eye. Their tooth formation may be delayed. This type of child will have more side effects from vaccinations.

Psychologically, they seem to lack the confidence to stand up for themselves, agreeing to everything that is said and getting easily discouraged. Although they lack self-confidence, they are quick minded and succeed in their undertakings. They are sure they are going to fail in their examinations, yet if they do perform them, they usually do very well. They have neat, clean, orderly minds with delicate perceptions. But they may have difficulties in concentrating, as the slightest noise hinders them. Their timidity will lead to performance anxiety, which makes them nervous and irritable. All of this will lead to physical and mental exhaustion due to overwork. They are weepy but they don't want consolation. They cry when scolded and when away from home get very homesick.

## The Nervous, Air Type

We will discuss two remedies in this category: Lycopodium and Natrum Muriaticum.

### 1. *The Lycopodium Child*

You all know one of those: an angel at school, a naughty child at home. Here is the child who is timid at school, with parents and older children, but who has no trouble being a bully towards younger children and animals, to whom he can be rather abusive. They talk to their younger siblings as if they are the parents, sounding haughty and dictatorial, but all this is just for show. These children suffer terribly from a low self-esteem, with deep hidden anxiety and melancholy. Their fear of failure can lead to stuttering, especially when confronted with new tasks or situations. This is in contradiction to their high degree of intelligence, their quick wit and sometimes violent fits of rage. When they wake up, like any liver type, they are in a foul mood, can't stand to be contradicted and refuse to go to school. These are children whose brains have developed at the expense of their bodies: they are lean with a possible pot belly, face and chest thinly covered with flesh but the legs are well developed. The eyes are sunken and surrounded by dark rings. They have cold legs, the right more than the left, and sometimes Lycopodium boys have an undescended right testicle. When they perspire, the sweat has an onion odor, and is most pronounced at the feet and under the armpits. They lack sympathy and warmth to be lovable. They are hypochondriacs and greedy.

They crave sweets, sugar, hot drinks and hot foods, but after only a few bites they can feel full. The quick fermentation leads to bloating, discomfort and abdominal swelling. They feel sleepy after meals and cannot tolerate any pressure from their clothes. They have constipation: there is dry stool, and the child always has the impression that there is more to come. They also suffer from recurrent colds and swollen glands with bursting headaches after doing their homework. They hate to be in hot, stuffy rooms, and in spite of being chilly, they are the first ones to throw the windows open. If you recognize your child as a Lycopodium type, it is important that he gets your support with the appropriate hygienic measures and homeopathy. If not, you will see this brilliant domineering type change into a miserable human being, both physically and emotionally.

### 2. *The Natrum Muriaticum (Nat-mur.) Child*

These children will inevitably get your sympathy. They are very quiet and reserved and are dragged into the physician's office by their mothers. They do not volunteer anything until after much coaxing by the doctor. Often, they are suffering from a silent grief, especially if the parents separated when the child was still young. They will hardly cry and give the impression that they don't care at all, but deep down, they care very much and would love sympathy. Yet they have a hard time showing it.

Nat-mur. children have difficulties in speech: they learn to talk late or they stay autistic, living in their own world. It would be interesting to see if many mothers of autistic children would have suffered from a heartbreaking situation, especially in the first three months of pregnancy. According to homeopathy, this can be reflected in the child, leading to this mysterious condition.

Although these children may look robust and fleshy, they are rather clumsy and easily tired. They are unable to differentiate the finer shades of meaning and they hate their school books, simply because they can't think or reason clearly. Exertion of the eyes and mind leads typically to a "school headache." This inability to analyze goes so far that they cannot learn how to play a musical instrument.

I remember a textbook case involving an Nat-mur. child. She was 18 years old, accompanied by her mother who was my patient. She sized me up, without volunteering to say anything. Short answers were given to my questions, and much information was relayed by the mother. Since I did not see the questionnaire that every patient fills out, I asked her where it was. She took it from her pocket -- she was hiding it from me, probably hoping I would not ask to see it. Upon questioning when her fatigue started, she told me about the heartbreak she had experienced five months ago. This, together with her external behavior, left no doubt about the remedy: Natrum Muriaticum would do wonders for this person.

In general a Nat-mur. child feels worse in the morning, at the seashore and upon being consoled. In spite of being chilly, she tolerates the heat very poorly, especially the sun. As she grows up, she wants to wear sunglasses all the time. Nat-mur. children crave salty foods like chips, pretzels, and popcorn and in general have a ravenous hunger, often leading to bulimia. They are very thirsty for cold drinks which they drink in big gulps. Very characteristically, these children don't want to go to the bathroom away from home; they are very self-conscious, shy, embarrassed and inhibited in the company of other people. Children need this remedy often for teenage melancholy around the onset of puberty: around that time, these children often exhibit psychic tiredness, lack of attentiveness, headaches and difficult social behavior.

## The Choleric Type

We will discuss two types: the Chamomilla child and the Nux Vomica (or junk food) child.

### 1. *The Chamomilla Child*

While you want to hug a Pulsatilla child, you want to spank a Chamomille child. While I will discuss the Pulsatilla child further, thousands and thousands of parents know exactly the meaning of these words.

The whole atmosphere surrounding the Chamomilla child gives the diagnosis away. They are snappy, irritable, hard to please and sure to drive you crazy. One moment they absolutely need 'that' object, only to hurl it away the next moment with a force that reflects the intensity of their inner spirit. Don't test the Chamomilla child too much or he will use bad language, become impolite and increase the gray hairs on his parents' heads. In an infant, this whole behavior can be triggered by teething, since the child experiences agony with pain and numbness. The tantrums typically start around 9 p.m. and last until midnight. Unless you have your homeopathic remedies ready, you are in for a tough night. Harsh words or reprimanding the Chamomilla child will not work. In his rage he will fall to the floor and won't stop screaming and squirming until you pick him up and rock him in your arms. The other solution is the nightly ride in the car: you strap the child in the car seat, drive around the block, and hope for a miracle. Often, Chamomilla will be asleep by the time you get home. But I would say to all parents that it is easier to have the homeopathic remedy at hand.

### 2. *The Nux Vomica Child*

This remedy, Nux Vomica, is the poison nut, and this in itself should warn you in advance for the types of encounters you will have with this angry little fellow. He wakes up in the morning in such a foul mood that no one dares to speak to Mr. Nux Vomica. It is much better to let him rage than to contradict him, which is like throwing fuel on the fire. Usually, it is a child who early in his life will discover the stimulating effects of coffee, drugs and alcohol.  Nux Vomica types have a tendency to lead a sedentary life, which, compounded by the intake of fats, fried foods and alcohol, easily leads to bloating, gas, abdominal discomfort and constipation.  (There is a frequent urge to defecate, but it is ineffective. The child has the feeling that part of the stool always remains in the intestines.)  He suffers from headaches and drowsiness after meals, which forces him to take a short nap.  There is a yellow-white coating on the middle of the tongue.  His sleep is very restless since he takes his hardships and school problems to bed.  He wakes up around 3 a.m. and finds himself thinking about what a mess he is in.

The Nux Vomica child can often be jealous of an older, more successful sibling.  (Especially if he has worked hard, but being less talented, sees other siblings reach goals where he should be.)  This disappointed ambition will be vented in quarrelings, scolding and insults.  He will not be cautious in his choice of words.  The more vulgar, the more it suits his mood. Nux Vomica girls will be tomboys: they have masculine, energetic and fiery tempers.  Throughout adulthood, most of their troubles will be linked to a wrong mode of living: overeating, drinking, and use of stimulants like coffee and other drugs, in addition to a lack of physical  exercise.

### Cold Phlegmatic Type

#### *The Pulsatilla Child*

This is the light skinned, blue-eyed, blond-haired child with the look of an angel.  She is usually introverted and seems always ready to cry. But the waterfall of tears which comes very easily will disappear once she is offered some sympathy. She switches from crying to laughing within seconds, driving her parents crazy with her changeable moods.  The child is mostly of an easy going, resigned nature.  She is down to earth, but don't let this fool you. She can harbor a good degree of passive irritability and stubbornness.  She will go to her room for days and brood but when the mother gives consolation and holds her in her arms, she easily gives in.

Being very shy, the Pulsatilla child dreads anything new; even thinking about her daily school chores can make her cry. She can be very prudish, hiding from strangers and awkward with the opposite sex. She can often get depressed, melancholic and despondent but once encouraged to go outside and play in the fresh air, she revives. All her moods are aggravated by being locked up in hot stuffy rooms, although she is clearly of the warm nature. While she often seems to be sleepy and exhausted during the day, in the evening she becomes wide awake and does not want to go to bed. Of course, in the morning she wakes up unrefreshed, after frequently talking in her sleep.

Healthwise, she catches one cold after another, with frequent formation of yellow, thick mucus. The mucus sometimes changes from clear to yellow, then to green and clear again. In spite of her dry mouth, she is rarely thirsty. Pulsatilla is called the puberty remedy: the Pulsatilla child will display the above-mentioned symptoms in an extreme degree around puberty. Many tears and fights could be saved by the wise application of this remedy. The Pulsatilla child craves ice cream, pastry and fried foods which, unfortunately, are poorly tolerated. Ingesting these foods invariably leads to bloating, difficult digestion and burping. All in all, the Pulsatilla child will be the spoiled, huggable member of the family, the child that does not want to grow up in this cruel world and needs the constant support of family or friends.

### The Sanguine Type

#### *The Bouncing Phosporus Child*

Think of phosphorescence: a glitter, a sprinkle of light, but no warmth. This is the quality that describes the extremely impressionable, creative, euphoric child. He loves to talk your ears off, shows interests in a million things, but because of a lack of physical stamina, is a wonderful beginner at tasks and a poor finisher. Usually this child is slender, with straw blond hair, freckles, is stoop-shouldered and has blue eyes. He is very psychic and intelligent.  In fact he is the most intelligent child but needs training and restraining because he can be excessive, disorderly and immodest in his intellectual conquests.  The bouncing Phosphorus child has grown up too fast and sticks out above anyone else in the class.  As bubbly as the Phosporus child is, there is a lot of fear, mainly of disease, the dark, and, typically, of storms.  He is a beautiful child with long eyelashes and eyes that captivate you within seconds.

But often the Phosphorus child can't follow this mental speed with physical strength.  He bounces between excitement and depression, between enthusiasm and disgust.  The child needs frequent short naps and seems to improve dramatically when he takes them. The Phosphorus child injures himself easily because he is very incautious.  Add to this the tendency of easy, spontaneous bruising, and you look at a child that seems to find his way through war zones.  The child is very thirsty, especially for large amounts of cold water, cooled down by many ice cubes. He loves ice cream, chocolate and salty treats like chips, pretzels and popcorn.  Besides the bruising, Phosporus tends to bleed easily everywhere.  Frequent nose bleeds, heavy menstrual flow (in a maturing female Phosphorus child), bleeding gums, etc. are characteristic.  This child needs frequent, small meals as there is a tendency toward hypoglycemia and food brings back his energy immediately.  He is very sensitive to light, noise, scents and touch.  These mentally bright but physically fragile children, susceptible and malleable, need guidance from their loved ones to attain a fullfilling life.  If so, they grow up to be passionate, warm people with powerful emotions, ready to help anyone they meet in life.

These are my homeopathic portraits of children. Once you know your child's type, it will give you and the homeopathic prescriber invaluable information.  If your child has the tendency to have recurrent, acute diseases such as ear infections, colds or sore throats after treatment of the acute disorder, a "constitutional" remedy will help to fight the susceptibility of that child for his or her particular weaknesses.

# SECTION TWO

## WHY DO YOU GET SICK?

## THE CAUSES OF DISEASE

# CHAPTER FOUR

## EMOTIONAL TRAUMA: THE STRONGEST CAUSATIVE FACTOR OF CHRONIC DISEASE

*"Those who say they have tested Homeopathy and it is a failure have only exposed their own ignorance"*

-- J.T. Kent, M.D.

Why is it that traditional Western medicine is so ill at ease with the treatment of chronic disease? Why are those patients with chronic illness so often referred to a psychiatrist? Why is it that the homeopathic physician can be very successful in treating chronically ill patients? Psychiatry and homeopathy share a common premise: that the patient is an individual, different and unique. For both the psychiatrist and the homeopathic physician, the whole of the patient is greater than the sum of all his or her parts.

A patient who assumes a chronically ill role needs to be evaluated as a person with physical and emotional needs, instead of being labeled "neurotic." For the alert physician, it means doing more than just jotting down a diagnosis of a pathology, and then giving out a prescription. A chronically ill person has anxieties, anger and depression because of built-up tensions. If the physician does not find a way to help that person release tension, to build up his or her self worth, then the physician has not helped at all. Mankind has major needs which, if not fulfilled, either directly cause his illness or are certainly major contributing factors to his dis-ease. Practitioners must consider these major needs of each individual at each interview. Failure to do so leads inevitably to the lingering on of the diseased state. What are those needs of mankind that the practitioner must address? Table 2 (page 59) lists these needs.

## Eight Needs of Mankind to Avoid Chronic Disease

### 1. Food, Shelter and Safety

The first major need is both physical and financial, related to the need for food, shelter and safety. Samuel Hahnemann, the founder of homeopathic medicine, states in his master work, *The Organon* (1810) that "those diseases are inappropriately named chronic which persons incur who expose themselves continually to avoidable noxious influences, who are in the habit of indulging in injurious liquors or aliments...These states of health, which persons bring upon themselves, disappear spontaneously under an improved mode of living, and they cannot be called chronic diseases."   Common sense dictates that unless the modern physician investigates his patient's living habits, he will limit himself to nothing more than dispensing bandaid therapy.  It is like giving cough syrup to a homeless person to treat his cold, but failing to address his lack of shelter and food as the maintaining causes of his cough.

### 2. Success

A second major need is that the chronically ill patient needs to succeed in an area important to him.  This is closely related to the inability of this patient to learn from his failures. Fear of failure prevents him from trying anything.  While a healthy person learns from his mistakes, these patients experience mistakes as a catalyst for a downward spiral in their health. The physician has to counsel and encourage his patient to set up reasonable goals and to try to reach them within a reasonable time period.

### 3. Mastery

A third major need is the ability to master a certain area. Every person, but especially one who is chronically ill, needs to find something he can do well. If he cannot succeed, what else is left but disease, despair -- or even worse, dishonesty and drug use? You are probably familiar with the rebellious teenager whose lack of mastery is turned into unacceptable behavior patterns. This disruptive behavior is at least getting him the much-needed attention at home or at school with his peers.

### 4. Recognition and Approval

Another major need, if unfulfilled, leads to continuance of chronic disease. This is the need for recognition and approval by those whom the patient feels are important in his life. Each person has a deep need for respect and appreciation by colleagues, husbands, wives and children for what the person is accomplishing, be it at work or at home. I know some of the most successful people in life who suffer from a chronic condition that is fueled by the absence of this recognition. These patients look for approval from their parents in what they have achieved in life, yet due to some misunderstanding or abuse in childhood, that recognition from their parents is never attained.

### 5. Affection, Love and Sympathy

A fifth major need is for affection, love and sympathy. There is a need to please and be pleased, to create a bond of affection that is related to emotional maturity. Sometimes, we physicians are persons of paid friendships. We are the home base away from home. We will listen without judgment, and provide the sympathy and warmth that may be lacking for the patient at home. It is music to our ears when the patient can claim after our initial consultation, "I feel so much better already!" No prescription will be successful without the demonstration of our genuine caring and friendship.

## 6. Security

A sixth major need is for security. Job security coupled with financial security eases many of our daily stresses. In every election, people let the candidates know that jobs are number one on their list of priorities. Security is at the very core of contentment, peace and happiness.

## 7. Creative Fulfillment

Another essential need is to fulfill one's creative impulses. Each person must have the freedom to follow his whims or desires, no matter how trivial they seem to be to others. To try a new adventure, to do an activity which gives a person a feeling of freedom from the monotony of daily routines, is as essential as our daily bread. And don't forget, we are all different. What will motivate one individual may have no effect on another. So don't downplay the creative desires of your partner. How often do we see in the absence of creative outlets a certain despair or anger; how often are drugs and alcohol used as alternatives?

## 8. Sexuality and Love

The eighth and sometimes forgotten and neglected need is for physical sexuality and love. Each person has a normal biological sexual need to be satisfied. We run into problems because these needs can be of a different magnitude or timing for different partners. Suppression of this need, exemplified in nuns and priests, leads to a decrease of the vital energy and opens the gate to chronic disease.

As you can see, it was much easier for the old-time physician who was doing house calls -- and who was much more a part of the family than his contemporary colleague is now -- to recognize the basic needs of his patients. In order for treatment to be successful, the modern physician will have to probe for these needs rather than suppress them by prescribing antidepressants and barbiturates drugs.

---

**TABLE 2**

**EIGHT NEEDS OF MANKIND**

- FOOD, SHELTER & SAFETY
- SUCCESS
- MASTERY
- RECOGNITION & APPROVAL
- AFFECTION, LOVE & SYMPATHY
- SECURITY
- CREATIVE FULFILLMENT
- SEXUALITY

---

## Neglected Emotional Factors

Modern medicine, with its strengths in pathology or germ knowledge, has tended to neglect psychological factors of disease. If it weren't for psychiatrists and psychotherapists, to whom the patients are referred after being declared "psychosomatic" by their physicians, the asylums would still be filled with "demons and witches." However, psychotherapists and psychiatrists can be just as out of touch as their counterparts, the "somatic" or "body" physicians.  They are only able to recognize the emotional symptoms, as if that were all there were to the patient. Very often, patients coming to my office have been declared "cured" from their grief and yet, because of my knowledge in alternative medicines, I can recognize the <u>physical</u> symptoms of grief in that patient, giving proof to the unfinished business of the psychotherapist.

Most of the emotional factors discussed in this chapter were recognized as important to the imbalance of organs as long ago as 5,000 years by the Chinese.  However, when it comes to balancing these factors and repairing their devastating effects, there is no medical approach more powerful than homeopathy. The number of remedies available to repair emotional damage is mind boggling.  Where psychiatry has about ten small pages of anti-psychotic drugs listed in the Physician's Desk Reference, homeopathy has at least a hundred pages of remedies, specifically designed and tailored to each patient. The next paragraphs will show you some of the treasure of homeopathic remedies for various emotional ailments and the homeopathic philosophy behind their use. You'll recognize many of the precipitating factors as the lack of one of the eight needs of mankind.

### Ailments from Hearing Bad News

Homeopathy has recognized the power of the word by providing a section or rubric in our repertory (the homeopathic symptom/remedy reference book)  entitled "Ailments from hearing bad news." But Western practitioners often act as if they have never heard about this concept.  I have often seen patients in my practice who were still traumatized by their doctors with this bad news ailment.  So often, we physicians play God and predict our patient's death as if we ourselves were able to let the curtain fall. Even worse, when lab tests show some abnormality that practitioners can't explain, they often demonstrate their "competence" by listing at least five deadly diseases as a possible diagnosis.  Once they have finally pinpointed the trouble, after the patient had to wait in agony for the news, then physicians usually blurt out the bad news, followed by what they think should be done.  "And if you don't do this, then surely you will die."  With these almighty words physicians are in control and patients are in shock, running around in a daze for the next 14 days, unable to pull themselves together.

What we physicians forget is that a harsh disclosure of a diagnosis and subsequent lack of empathy and information lead to emotional stress which suppresses the immune system.  Fear is a common cause of sickness.  Those patients who are fearful are likely to become sick; but those who face disease with courage and a fighting spirit are likely to remain well.  Have you ever thought about the fact that some physicians, although exposed to epidemics of an infectious disease, remain uninfected? They are so busy with the act of caring for people that they have no time to have fear: they are largely protected simply because they love their work.

Some of the best homeopathic remedies for "ailments from hearing bad news" are Gelsemium and Ignatia. The patient in need of Gelsemium is in a daze, unable to do anything. He feels flat, down, drowsy, or sleepless, and the smallest physical or emotional effort is impossible. The patient in need of Ignatia often reacts to the "bad news" with the words, "I can't believe this happened to me." He becomes depressed, sad, tearful and melancholic with uncontrollable sighing. It is as if he has fallen into a deep hole from which he sees no escape. He feels weak with an emptiness in the pit of his stomach, waking up at night battling with the unresolved problem.

One of the common questions in case management is always "Shall the doctor tell the patient if they have a serious disease?" A wise man once said, "When it's time for them to know, they will know and tell *you*. After that you can discuss it with them." But for the physician's protection if one is sure about the diagnosis a near relative should be told. Just as with many other factors in the practice of medicine, disclosure of difficult diagnoses is an art. Modern physicians would do well to return to some of the art practiced by their forebears, the family doctor.

### Ailments from a Broken Heart

Who has never experienced the agony of rejected love? Who has never felt the dagger of betrayal and felt afterwards that life was not worth living? Very few among us have escaped it and yet often we fail to see the ill-making effects of this heartbreaking event. The more sensitive among you go to a psychotherapist and try to mend your broken heart with countless hours of therapy. Alas! Sometimes I see this patient come to my office after such a "supportive" psychotherapeutic consultation in tears, upset and clearly down physically and emotionally. It is sufficient to refer to my nine points of health in Chapter One to know that this therapy has not been very helpful. A more skillful therapist would have proceeded at a level and pace that were tolerable for the client. It is difficult for the therapist to know when her therapy has been helpful and health has been achieved. Perhaps she thinks she can perceive with her intellect when a "cure" has been achieved. A homeopathic physician would look for the physical symptoms of grief, such as:

- cravings for salty things
- eye sensitivity to sunlight
- dry skin with oily forehead
- thirst for cold drinks
- chilliness
- feeling of a lump in the throat
- skin diseases such as psoriasis, urticaria (hives) and acne
- recurrent herpes attacks
- loss of weight and fatigue
- headaches from prolonged mental work
- learning disabilities
- bulimia or anorexia nervosa behaviors
- greasy hair
- dryness of the mucosae (lips, mouth)
- painful intercourse (vaginism)
- infertility
- late development of speech in children
- PMS with irritability and water retention

There are many grief remedies and you should consult a homeopathic physician for further help. Ignatia for an acute heartbreak and Natrum Muriaticum for chronic grief are wonderful remedies. They will help resolve the grief quickly and gently and will be of a tremendous help along with psychotherapy.

### Ailments from Nursing Loved Ones

Nursing a loved one is also called night watching. A family member suffers from a chronic, incurable disease and is cared for at home. The caretaker's life will be dominated by the patient's needs. Sleep is constantly interrupted by the needs of the patient. The caretaker's sleep becomes restless and light because they fear they won't hear their ill partner call for help. Before they know it, these caretakers are suffering from chronic insomnia. It is only the enormous and sometimes thankless task that keeps them going, but once the partner has expired, the caretaker feels as if he or she has gone through the wringer.

If this description of a life situation fits you, you may feel weak and nauseated and suffer from recurrent attacks of dizziness. You have the feeling that your neck is incapable of holding your head up, that your back and knees are collapsing. You have a "sinking" feeling and a metallic taste in your mouth. You have an empty feeling throughout your whole body. You become a twilight sleeper: you have no recollection of having slept and you wake up unrefreshed. While this loss of sleep is caused by taking care of a sick friend or relative day and night over a long period, other life situations create similar circumstances. I have seen patients lose their health because of sleepless nights caused by the crying newborn. Or the student who, by lack of foresight, has to study through the night. And then there is the jet traveler, who zooms from one continent to another, unmindful of the ravages that the time difference creates on his body. All of these people put themselves at risk for chronic disease through the lack of sleep they experience. Some homeopathic prescriptions are Cocculus, Phosphorus and Causticum.

### Ailments from Guilt Feelings and Indignation

We all know the unfortunate victims of physical, emotional and verbal abuse. Statistics of the abuse of children in the U.S. are horrifying. For many of these unfortunate souls, the abuse may last a lifetime. Abused children often stay with what they know by marrying an abusive partner. The shame of their past creates the low self-worth that stops them from standing up against the abuse. They wilt under confrontation and when they are assaulted, they are often too numb to react. This is a common ailment for a rape victim whose dignity has been taken away. These patients have bottled up anger: the slightest word offends them and irritates them beyond normal limits. There is a mental dullness, a pathological desire to please, a fear of sex and of members of the opposite sex. The following physical symptoms can be a consequence of suffering such an indignation:

- recurrent bladder infections ("honeymoon cystitis")
- vaginism (painful intercourse)
- frequent need to urinate, every hour
- acute and chronic prostatitis
- styes on the upper eyelids
- eczema of the face
- ulcerative colitis
- recurrent vaginitis and yeast infections

An excellent homeopathic remedy to address the effects of abuse is Staphysagria, sometimes called the "rape" remedy (See Chapter Eleven).

### Ailments from Anticipation

Have you ever heard of those cases where the patient does not dare to leave his house because of fear that "something is going to happen?" Usually, this phobia leads to diarrhea, supplying a justification for the patient to stay at home. We know of all kinds of phobias: of heights (acrophobia), of elevators, or other enclosed places (claustrophobia), of going to public places (agoraphobia), and many other fears -- of flying, crowds, public speaking, death, being alone, going to the dentist, poverty, failing in business, men, people, losing self-control, etc.

All these phobias can be grouped together under the fear of "impending doom." Typically, the patient ponders the question: "What if?" What if I do this, what is going to happen? This leads to irrational behavior, dwelling on the future and a constantly excited, hurried mode of living. They experience brainfag with mild mental exertion, while they are driven to do everything quickly. They crave sugar, sweets and chocolate and consume them in huge quantities. Physical symptoms are emotionally-induced diarrhea, recto-colitis, stomach ulcers and severe conjunctivitis. Excellent homeopathic remedies are Argentum Nitricum, Gelsemium (#1 remedy for fear of the dentist) and Aconite.

## Ailments from Lost Ambition and Disappointment

I remember very well such a case in my practice. The patient was a very well-known actress whose year had been so brilliant that everyone predicted an Oscar nomination for her that year. And indeed, she was nominated. Prior to the awards ceremony, friends and producers had already predicted her winning, so that in her mind, that evening was going to be the fulfillment of all her dreams. When the award went to another actress, it was as if her world had been taken away from her. She didn't even remember how she got home that night. She slept for two full days, unable to bring herself to do her daily chores. After this, she suffered from Chronic Fatigue with all of its morbid symptoms.

Since this woman had never received her mother's approval, winning this Oscar would, at least in her eyes, have redeemed her with her mother. Her ambition was taken away from her when her big plans did not go through. This example alone should teach us doctors that CFIDS (Chronic Fatigue and Immune Dysfunction Syndrome) is not caused by an unidentified virus. In this particular case, Lycopodium repaired much of the harm that Oscar night had done to her, with a gradual resolving of most of her symptoms. There was no strange virus causing her disease. Of course, the enormity of the emotional shock decreased her vital energy to the point where infections could easily take hold.

The physical symptoms of lost ambition are:

- cravings for sweets and sugar
- cravings for fresh air and dread of closed, stuffy places
- bloating below the navel
- constipation with the feeling of ineffectual urges to defecate
- premature gray hair
- easy satiety: full after a few mouthfuls
- cravings for warm drinks and foods
- discomfort with tight clothes around the waist
- liver pains

- migraines of digestive origin
- slow digestion (digestive enzymes are needed)
- premature ejaculations and soft erections

### Ailments Due to Business Failure

Remember the stock market crash of October 1987? Countless victims committed suicide, not being able to cope with the loss of their life savings. Others went into deep depression. For these victims, this was all they had left: their plan for a wonderful, carefree retirement. Almost surely, whoever lost heavily in those days was never the same. I saw several patients in my office and remember their despair, hopelessness and grief. Many came down with CFIDS, joining its ranks of millions of victims. This brutal, sudden shock, which robbed people of their security and instilled fear of poverty, was intense enough to suppress their immune systems. You can imagine that treating these patients with anti-viral drugs would not be enough to repair the damage. These patients are very irritable, easily angered, depressed, melancholic and sometimes suicidal. They are restless, always in a hurry, or are quietly pacing the floor. It is as if they have lost all meaning in life. They desire coffee and liqueurs and often have an increased appetite. The allopathic physician would probably prescribe antidepressants. In homeopathy, the remedy is Aurum Metallicum, which is nothing but the metal gold. Gold, which symbolizes wealth and financial security, has helped countless victims recover from this depression.

### Ailments Due to Emotional Excitement

When you get sick, you often think about all the negative stressors you've experienced. But not only negative stimuli deplete your vital energy. Even positive events such as a marriage, expecting a baby or a promotion at work can be the trigger to chronic disease. I remember a case in which the woman got married, moved to another state and got a new job, all at the same time. The occurrence of several stressful events, although positive, proved too much for this patient. For the next several months, she experienced severe fatigue, brainfag and immense cravings for sweets. This is not an isolated case. Often the occurrence of several trigger factors at the same time proves to be too much for the immune system.

Sometimes if there is one big positive excitement these patients exhibit cerebral hyperactivity. There is an onrush of ideas, optimism and euphoria at first, as if the patient is on amphetamines or coffee. All the senses are acute: she hears better, becomes sensitive to odors and becomes more sensitive to pain. Her restless mind will keep her busy at night, leading to insomnia. The patient is so excited about everything going on in her life that she cannot fall asleep. Inevitably this will lead to a nervous breakdown. She will become moody, jumping from being happy one moment to crying the next. This sensorial hyperactivity, this hyperactive mind, makes us think about the effects of caffeine. It is not surprising that homeopathy has found the right remedy by potentizing coffee: homeopathic Coffea is given with excellent results to this type of patient.

## Ailments Due to Lack of Self-Confidence

I have seen many cases of chronic illness that were caused by a lack of self-confidence. This lack of self-confidence can have numerous sources. I have seen it in patients who had high hopes for their future plans, but when they failed, their confidence faded away with it. Others were rejected by their parents or their loved ones; some were put down at work and humiliated in front of their co-workers. And social non-acceptance, related to sex, race, religion or economic class, leads again to a feeling of low worth. Others have to struggle with a physical handicap, making it impossible to achieve their goals. It is this sustained, insidious stress that robs patients of their vitality. It might not be as clear as a single, severe emotional trauma, but the effects will be the same. These people will procrastinate at everything: they start many things, yet finish none. As an excuse, they tell you that they got bored. In reality, they have performance anxiety, can't make decisions, and experience fear of failure and rejection. They are very timid and are overly concerned with their appearance, paying attention to minute details. One of the nicest remedies in homeopathy is Lycopodium, already discussed under "Ailments from lost ambition."

### Ailments from Loneliness

Don't neglect this factor. With an increased divorce rate and decreasing numbers of marriages, it is bound to touch many among you. Growing up in an alcoholic family, in abusive environments or simply in an alienating world, will zap more physical and emotional energy from you than you think. When you are lonely, you feel abandoned, estranged, helpless, empty and resentful. Nobody seems to care about you, which intensifies that deep feeling of loneliness. You are sad and cry easily, looking for a glimpse of sympathy and consolation. Whenever you do find sympathy, you immediately feel better. You are undecided and unresolved, shy and prudish. Foods -- especially fatty foods, pastries and carbohydrates -- are your only consolation. You have extremely strong maternal instincts and love children, but since you have no partner, this deep sentiment is unfulfilled. Pulsatilla is the homeopathic gem that has saved many patients from this forsaken feeling.

### Ailments from Jealousy

Oh, the almighty burning fire of jealousy! It kills every wonderful feeling, alienates you from your loved ones, and makes life impossible for everyone, especially you. Where does it come from? Frequently from a disappointed love, sometimes from a grief or poor confidence. Whatever it is, it makes you possessive, especially in relationships. You are insecure, selfish, arrogant and easily offended. You have a strong imagination and anticipate that everything will go wrong because you have a deep-seated fear that something is going to happen.

You have no trust and there is an intense desire for revenge. You think, "If I can't have him (or her), no one can!" There is a tendency to be manic depressive. In your downswings, you feel hateful, feeling that people are constantly saying bad things about you, that you are being cheated and that everyone hates you. You have a smoldering anger, which makes you explode at a moment's notice. You are very loquacious, talking at random, jumping from one subject to another. Your hot-bloodedness just brings you more isolation and loneliness. In Chinese medicine, this jealousy is believed to disrupt the energy in your liver, leading to hypertension, insomnia, irritability, palpitations, heart disease and alcoholism. Western medicine has a hard time with these patients but homeopathy has many excellent remedies, among which Lachesis is tops.

### Ailments from Home-Sickness

Sometimes parents may think it is in the best interests of their children to send them away at an early age to boarding school. "It is good for your future, it is the best school around," they say. But often they forget that the child might be too shy, still depends a lot on the parents, or just is trying to find his niche in this world. And while this might not cause any harm in some, for many struggling with this feeling of abandonment leads to melancholy. One case comes to mind. This patient came down with breast cancer at age 35. Carefully exploring her past, I found out that at age twelve she had been sent overseas because she had won a scholarship. She stayed there for three lonely years, as she expressed it, longing to be with her family. In the highly competitive environment of her model school, she never could make friends, and there was no time for vacations. Telling me this story, she still cried, 20 years later! Afterwards, upon her return to the U.S., her health became fragile and she later was diagnosed with breast cancer. I have no doubt that her homesickness contributed to the suppression of her immune system. The homeopathic remedy Phosphoric Acid proved to be a savior for her. It repaired her grief and fatigue and lifted her spirits.

This list of emotional triggers is by no means complete. But by highlighting some of these emotions, I hope to draw the attention, of the public and professionals alike, to the often forgotten link between illness and emotions. I have seen all of the above triggers in my practice, especially in CFIDS patients. It is important to assist patients in their immediate crises such as the ones just described, and to repair the damage before the loss of vital energy becomes enormous and <u>allows</u> diseases to form. I know of no better form of medicine capable of doing this than homeopathy. We, as homeopathic physicians, have an array of simple, inexpensive remedies at our disposal that deal with the whole person, not just parts of his or her body.

# CHAPTER FIVE

# HEREDITARY FACTORS AND MIASMS: THE SEAT OF ALL CHRONIC DISEASES?

*"The disease is not to be named, but to be perceived; not to be classified, but to be viewed, that the very nature of it may be discovered."*
--- J.T. Kent, M.D.

### The Biggest Sin of Western Medicine

*Suppression* refers to treatment of a single symptom while neglecting the symptom totality. While true homeopathy stands or falls on the concept of the totality (See Chapter Eight), modern medicine more often than not concentrates on the treatment of single symptoms. In Western medicine, suppression would refer to the removal of surface symptoms, skin eruptions and discharges from mucous membranes (vaginal, bronchial, urethral, etc.). But what is actually occurring when we treat only superficial symptoms? I have often encountered women suffering from recurrent vaginal yeast infections whose only treatment consisted of the suppression of the discharge. After being prescribed all the different creams and suppositories, these victims still experienced recurrences and were virtually abandoned by their doctors, who labeled them as hysterical. Because their physicians were only treating surface symptoms, and not the underlying cause, the sign of dis-ease kept coming back. Only after treatment with the indicated homeopathic remedy did these women finally experience relief.

People with skin eruptions can sometimes be even bigger victims. I remember a case of a sweet lady with a violent rash covering both her legs. She could not sleep because of the burning and itching. After cortisone shots and creams for one and a half years, ten different dermatologists whom she consulted gave up on her. But an adjusted diet and the appropriate homeopathic remedy made the burning and itching disappear in one day, and the remainder of the rash went away in another month.

Another elderly lady consulted me for burning, day and night, of both feet. For years, the most eminent dermatology professors couldn't figure out what was causing her malady. It took only one consultation to choose the right homeopathic remedy, according to the totality of the symptoms, and she was cured. I never had to treat her again. One month later, she and her husband came to thank me for this true "miracle."

The idea that the cure comes, through elimination, from the inside out is as old as medicine itself. The Chinese understood this concept very well almost 5,000 years ago. And modern research (Woodruff and Carrel) has demonstrated that single cell organisms could be kept alive in a nutritional fluid if the waste products of their metabolism were removed through regular washing and replacement of the solution. The process of elimination of toxic products is of life-saving, prime importance. In the disease process, toxic products accumulate to an extent greater than is normal. What homeopathy does is to access the body's own system for flushing out toxins by stimulating the excretory organs to accomplish what they normally do when the body is well. In a normal state, the excretory organs of the body accomplish a "washing out" -- with the help of the "periphery" -- skin, mucous membranes, excretory organs (vagina, urinary system, bronchial system, gastrointestinal system), the body rids itself of the toxic products. Homeopathy, in treating the totality of the symptoms, helps stimulate the body to do a total "washing out" in order to finish the cure.

By suppressing a skin eruption or discharge, modern Western medicine can actually do more harm than good. Each time we suppress one of these symptoms, we drive the disease inwards towards the more precious internal organs. The only good therapy is to accelerate the "exteriorization," so that the body can flush out the toxins itself.

In his masterwork, the 6th edition of the *Organon*, Hahnemann warns us of this unnatural act of suppression. In Paragraph 201, he writes:

*"The local affection, however, is never anything else than a part of the general disease, a part transferred to a less dangerous [external] part of the body...."*

and in Par. 202:

*" If the old-school physician* [read: modern doctor] *should now destroy the local symptom by the topical application of external remedies* [our creams and suppositories], *under the belief that he thereby cures the whole disease, Nature makes up for it by rousing the internal malady and the other symptoms that previously existed in a latent state side by side with the local affection; that is to say, <u>she increases the internal disease.</u>"*

These words of wisdom were written 200 years ago. The *Los Angeles Times* (December, 1992) carried an article about the "discovery" of modern medicine, that suppression of fever is not favorable and that intake of Tylenol$^{(TM)}$ increases the length of many childhood diseases. To understand more about how the homeopathic theory of chronic disease can be helpful in our modern world, let's take a look at Hahnemann's groundbreaking work in this area.

## Understanding Chronic Disease

In 1817, Cuvier studied the animal kingdom inasmuch as it was known then, and classified all animal life into four great kingdoms: the Vertebrates, Mollusks, Articulates and Radiates. Samuel Hahnemann, a contemporary of Cuvier, faced an even more enormous task when he undertook the classification of disease. Medicine was at that time in a very chaotic condition, and little was known of disease beyond a few names. Even to his scientific mind, this was a Herculean task. Hahnemann observed that although homeopathy was effective in eradicating acute diseases (even epidemics), many difficulties were encountered in the treatment of chronic disease. Initially, patients responded to the homeopathic remedies, but they later ceased to do so, and either the same or new symptoms reappeared. And these new symptoms were harder to eradicate.

Hahnemann did not take his task lightly. For the next ten years, he went through thousands of his patient files and tried to identify a common cause for chronic disease. He came up with a theory of chronic diseases in 1816 that even created controversy among his peers: the miasm theory. With this theory, Hahnemann achieved then what contemporary medicine still struggles with today: the understanding that, in many instances, an acute illness is only the tip of the iceberg and failure to correct the underlying weakness amounts to nothing more than bandaid therapy.

## Hahnemann's Classification of Chronic Disease

As Cuvier classified animal life into four kingdoms, so Hahnemann classified disease into four great divisions. The first classification was relatively simple: it embraced all disease conditions that might spring from mechanical or exterior sources and that might be rectified by regulating habits and environment. These conditions were largely self-curative when the environment and habits were properly regulated. In fact, Hahnemann did not consider these diseases chronic, but believed that an inferior lifestyle transformed acute conditions into chronic ones.

Hahnemann was the first physician who paid so much attention to hygiene. He taught his peers and patients that some disease conditions were dependent entirely on external conditions, and he encouraged the removal of these conditions as the first step in the proper method of cure. When Hahnemann was called for consultation at the bedside of one of another doctor's patients, the first thing he would do was draw open the curtains, open the windows for fresh air and at the same time, throw any worthless medications out of the window. It was the accepted practice during this period of history to lock up sick people in dark, stuffy rooms. They would also get purgatives, depleting their vital fluids. Additionally, so much blood was tapped from them that the poor souls, weakened by these barbaric methods, would finally stop complaining and cease being restless. They would get increasingly weak as their "doctors" hastened their deaths.

The next three classifications of chronic disease fell under the heading of miasms. The term (from the Greek, meaning *"taint, contamination, pollution or stigma"*) was already in use at the time, but Hahnemann gave an entirely new meaning to the word. Hahnemann's central idea was that every chronic disease begins with the introduction into the organism of one of the contaminating agents -- miasms -- through the skin. So the first sign of disease is a skin lesion. When the contaminating agent is then "driven inwards" by misguided allopathic treatment, it becomes established throughout the organism and becomes a chronic condition. A class example is the modern treatment which causes the alternation between eczema and asthma. Aggressive treatment of eczema often leads to asthma attacks. The asthma is then treated and the skin symptoms come back.

For Hahnemann, there were three miasms, or stigmata, responsible for all chronic diseases: he called them *psora*, (pronounced SORE-ah), *sycosis and syphilis*. Modern homeopaths have added two more miasms: cancer and tuberculosis, which will be discussed later. Reading the descriptions of these miasms and their symptoms will give you a clue as to why some diseases keep on recurring and why modern medicine does not have an answer to many mysterious diseases.

### Psora, the Mother of All Miasms

In medical dictionaries, psora is defined as scabies or "the itch." But to link psora exclusively with scabies is a considerable over-simplification -- something even orthodox homeopathic physicians are guilty of doing. Psora is also bacterial and fungal. In Hahnemann's time, scabies was rampant. It is no surprise, then, that according to Hahnemann, psora was considered the foundation of human illness responsible for seven-eighths of all chronic diseases (the remainder were believed to be due to sycosis and syphilis). While almost everyone is familiar with the contagiousness of syphilis and gonorrhea, most do not know that psora is much more contagious than syphilis, and can be spread -- especially to children -- simply by touching the skin. In this day and age, nearly everyone is psoric to some degree. While the symptoms of psora occupied about 33 pages in Hahnemann's *Chronic Diseases*, I will discuss some of the more common ones. Many of you will recognize some of the signs of this miasm.

Skin symptoms play a major role in the expression of this miasm. The skin is itchy, hot and burning, either with or without eruptions. Itching is relieved by scratching, and becomes worse in the evening, under a warm shower and in the heat of the bed. The skin is dry, rough, sometimes unhealthy looking. The hair is dry and dull.

Psychological symptoms of psora include moodiness and impressionability. These patients can be hypersensitive to environmental factors and can be chronic complainers who feel they never will get well. They can be lazy and apathetic. Other symptoms of this miasm are vertigo, car sickness, headaches upon awakening in the morning and cravings for sweets and seasoned, rich, and fried foods. Typically there is drowsiness and bloating after meals, and more constipation than diarrhea. There is tingling and numbness in the extremities and the patient hates standing because this makes him tired. Palms and soles can become hot especially at night and quite often there is a disagreeable odor from the feet.

In general, symptoms that indicate a deficiency, a hypo ["low"] function or a lack of function, are characteristic of psora.

### Sycosis, the Fig-Wart Disease

The second miasm got its popular name from the presence of warty growths on the sexual organs. While there is much more to sycosis than these warts, the condylomata lata, as we call them in modern medicine, are a sure signature of sycosis. According to Hahnemann, this miasm is due to suppressed gonorrhea. Usually, acute inflammation of the genital tract occurs five days after infection; most cases are treated with suppressive drugs which drive the trouble inward, producing the state of miasm. Thus, so-called "cured" husbands can then pass this on to their wives who begin to feel unwell and the result is the transmission of secondary gonorrhea. I have seen many female patients in my practice whose troubles started only after they got married. They never felt well again as they presented with recurrent yeast or bladder infections and often were pronounced as "allergic" to their husbands. But this only demonstrates how the sycotic miasm is transferred from one partner to another. Sycosis is not the same as what was once called "the clap" (slang for gonorrhea, a venereal disease) or *Tripperseuche* in German. The latter is a local infection of the urinary organs with urethral pus formation. These previously mentioned condylomata occurred in people who had never had gonorrhea. But most probably, in all those cases too, intercourse with an infected person had probably taken place.

The sycotic patient is cross, irritable and suspicious. He is jealous, broods easily and can be devoid of any sense of righteousness. Vicious individuals, thieves and murderers are the products of sycosis. In sysosis, vesicular eruptions, as seen in herpes simplex infections and impetigo, are characteristic. Profuse perspiration that does not relieve the patient, diarrhea with sour smelling stools following dietary indiscretion, severe spastic colon, hemorrhoids with intense itching and infections in the pelvic cavity (pelvic inflammatory disease or P.I.D.) with extreme dysmenorrhea (painful and uncomfortable menstruation) are all signs of sycosis. The soles of the patient's feet are painful and the patient often has the feeling of walking on cobbles. All his symptoms are worsened by dampness, a condition to which this patient is very sensitive. Asthma, especially the humid type which is hereditary, is a purely sycotic manifestation, and is often aggravated between 2 a.m. and 3 a.m.

In general, we can say that symptoms which express a hyper function, a hyperplasia, or an exteriorization such as warts, polyps and cysts, manifest sycosis.

### Syphilis, the Come-Back Illness

The third miasm, syphilis, seems well on its way towards making a comeback, equal to or surpassing the peaks of infection right after World War II.

As is common in modern medicine, physicians often assume that the disease is localized at the onset of the infection with the appearance of a chancre on the genital organs. However, syphilis is systemic, affecting the entire body's system from the onset and not merely confined to the chancre. So simply treating this lesion is not only ineffective but harmful, and the disease will continue to produce subsequent manifestations. Even treatment with antibiotics will not eliminate the underlying miasm. Eye infections (keratitis and iritis) frequently occur, even leading to perforation of the cornea. Eyebrows and eyelashes fall out, and ulceration in the mouth, gums and tonsils often troubles the syphilis patient. A metallic taste in the mouth always suggests the syphilitic miasm. Severe headaches and bone pains that are worse at night and laryngeal infections are other chief manifestations of the syphilitic miasm.

Emotionally, the syphilitic miasm leads to dullness of the mind, depression, and anxiety, especially at night. Children who inherit this miasm will have the "old man" appearance typical of this condition and tend to exhibit destructive behavior. They will bite, hit, kick and their violent nature will lead them to break things and behave with cruelty towards animals and other human beings. They are obstinate, headstrong, restless, and have periods of rage during which they show increased strength. They often dwell on morbid things like death, incarceration, and murder. These unfortunate children are often labeled hyperactive by their physicians.

In general, symptoms that express the miasm syphilis include those of a destructive temperament.

### Miasm Theory's Significance Today

There is no doubt that if Hahnemann were still alive, he would considerably expand his theory of miasm. Hahnemann was 77 years old when he produced this theory and simply ran out of time. With the knowledge of modern pathology today, it would be hard not to make the connection between miasms and infective agents. But the projection of yet another miasm, cancer, shows that not all chronic disease is linked to infection. Indeed, modern homeopaths have added two other miasms to the three existing ones: tuberculosis (TB) and cancer. For many practicing homeopaths, the latter two are considered mixed miasms. The TB miasm, for instance, is a mixture of psora and syphilis. The incidence of the miasms has also changed. Remember, in Hahnemann's time seven-eighths of the miasms were psora. Today, the most prescribed miasms are, in order of frequency of occurrence:

- **Sycosis**
- **Cancer**
- **Tuberculosis**
- **Psora**
- **Syphilis**

As you can see, sycosis has become the more predominant miasm of our modern times. One contributing factor is the continuous suppressive therapy we are giving to its victims, allowing the "stigma" to be transferred to sexual partners. Suppose we have a man suffering from gonorrhea. Modern medicine will suppress the clinical symptoms and the patient gets the green light to be sexually active again. The disease can then be transferred to his partner in the <u>same stage</u> at which it existed in the man at the time of transference. This is equally true of the three other miasms: the disease is transferred from partner to partner and is taken up in the stage at which it existed, to progress from there. This is not <u>always</u> the case, as can be explained by the law of <u>law of dissimilar diseases.</u> This law states that "two dissimilar diseases repel each other." This would mean that a person only stays free from the infecting miasm if there is a disease present in his or her body that is so severe and overwhelming that there is "no place" for a lesser virulent condition like syphilis or gonorrhea.

Clinical manifestations of sycosis in our modern times are well-known. They range from recurrent yeast infections, bladder infections, genital warts, HPV (human papilloma virus), recurrent herpes simplex attacks, to AIDS.  The latter is often a mixed miasm with the three original miasms present.  As you can see from the previous explanation, a simple anti-viral or anti-yeast therapy will be insufficient.  The stigma or miasm has to be removed.  This is only possible through an anti-miasmic remedy, chosen according to the strictest homeopathic rules (See Chapter Eight).

I once treated a case of sycotic miasm in a 15 year-old girl, who underwent a thyroidectomy because of papillary carcinoma (cancer).  While operating, her doctors found a severe inflammation (a "hyper" condition) of the total gland.  No plausible cause could be detected in the patient's or the mother's history.  The only resolution was total removal of the thyroid, followed by replacement therapy.  For Western medicine this was the end of the story.  But for the concerned patient and her parents, this was just the beginning of their worries.  Why did this happen in an apparently healthy teenager?  What would she need to do to prevent a relapse of cancer and immune suppression in the future?  Western medicine drew a blank, but a careful questioning from a homeopathic perspective brought the diagnosis of sycotic miasm forward.

From that point on, it was easy:  The number one remedy for sycosis (and also for thyroid tumors) is Thuja.  It is easy to see in this case that the sycotic miasm was probably latent for several generations -- since the family could not remember any incidence of either gonorrhea or thyroid cancer in the family -- and the dormant miasm surfaced in this 15 year-old patient (although we still don't know why).  Most importantly, prescription of an anti-miasmatic remedy should clear up this miasm, preventing other related diseases from surfacing.

### Modern Explanation of Psora

As explained before, behind all chronic diseases is the presence of one of three possible "poisons": syphillis, sycosis, or psora.  No chronic disease can be cured unless the deep poison behind it is dealt with; failing such treatment, the most that one can hope for is a relief of recurrent symptoms.  While we can define syphilis and sycosis bacteriologically, what is psora in modern language?

To clarify the term psora and link it to modern bacteriology, I have used the 5,000 year old healing art, acupuncture, as a bridge. In acupuncture, the skin is related to the lung organ. The lung together with the large intestine form the Yin/Yang unity, the Yang being the exterior or superficial part and related to the skin, and the Yin being related to the deeper organ, or large intestine. The skin eruption can be seen as an external manifestation of an internal organ imbalance. In the case of psora, with its many related skin symptoms, I draw the hypothesis that psora is the manifestation of the internal disorder in the large intestine, whose connection and unity with the skin is well-known in Eastern philosophy. This would be the bridge linking Psora to modern bacteriology and the theory forwarded by Edward Bach, an eminent bacteriologist of England, who around 1920 related intestinal toxemia to many chronic diseases. Dr. Bach was a bacteriologist before becoming a homeopath and was astonished at the insight Hahnemann had already without the help of a microscope. Using a third medical modality, acupuncture, <u>I can state with certainty that many aspects of Psora are covered by intestinal toxemia.</u> What are the practical therapeutic consequences?

In general, diet to which civilized mankind has accustomed itself renders the alimentary tract, particularly the colon, a ready breeding ground for Gram-negative, non-lactose fermenting bacilli like Gaertner, Morgan, proteus and so forth. In modern medicine, these organisms are considered non-pathogenic, basically because they cause no symptoms in laboratory animals and they can be present for long periods of time in human beings without causing obviously associated disease. Why, may you ask, if they are important in our eyes as pathogenic organisms, is disease not always demonstrable? The answer is that the immediate virulence of these bacteria is small, and our bodies, starting with a reasonable amount of health, can face toxins for years without apparent inconvenience. But in time the persistence of their toxins makes up for its relatively slight virulence. The results are that these generalized toxemias will be the driving force behind many chronic degenerative diseases.

This intestinal toxemia will target the weakest tissue first causing an array of different chronic diseases in different people: M.S., ulcerative colitis, rheumatoid arthritis, and cancers can all be linked to it.

Intestinal toxemia is not a new idea. From the earliest records of medicine we find evidence that it was consciously or unconsciously recognized, as evidenced by the drugs and remedies used by the earliest physicians. But diet in general has undergone dramatic changes. Originally, our intestinal tract was made to digest the raw, natural ingredients found in nature. Over the centuries it has developed to a diet mainly consisting of cooked, modified ingredients, artificially colored and preserved. Has it ever occurred to you what difference there is between the content of the large intestine of an individual living on raw food and one living on cooked food? Civilized people with their cooked food have stool that is foul in odor, dark, and alkaline in reaction. The bacterial content is mainly composed of Bacillus coli, streptococci and yeast cells. The healthy, raw food eating dieter has a colon content with no odor, light in color and slightly acidic in character. The bacterial content consists of the lactic acid bacilli (our popular acidophilus!) with some Bacillus Coli. The healthy acidity content of the colon depends on the growth of the lactic acid bacillus, which needs starch to ensure its multiplication. However, ordinary forms of starch or simple carbohydrates (potatoes) are converted to sugar long before they reach the colon and fail to feed the good bacilli. Complex carbohydrates such as nuts and oatmeal are convenient means of supplying a starch that remains largely unconverted to sugar in the upper part of the bowel. Considering the varying diets of people throughout the world, it is one of Nature's marvels that the human race is not extinct yet. But the penalty is disease and degeneration.

What does this theory of intestinal toxemia, then, have to offer to humankind? I do not believe, as is clear from the contents of this book, that the bacteria are the cause of the disease, but rather the result. However, the mere continous presence is toxic enough for human organisms to cause a breach in the defenses and cause a breakdown of health. Dr. Bach, after performing stool cultures, made vaccines, or nosodes. He used the different bacteria found in the patient to make up a vaccine, according to homeopathic standards, not modern Western ones. Either he used the bacteria from the patient himself *(autogenous preparation)* or more often used the nosode composed of collected organisms of hundreds of patients, *(polyvalent nosode)* mixing together and potentized.  It has done wonders for many patients with "incurable," chronic conditions.  It does not replace homeopathy, but rather is another weapon for the homeopathic physician when confronted with a case in which it is difficult to find the exact homeopathic remedy.  Whether these organisms are the cause or result of disease, they are associated with chronic conditions.  The nosode will purify the patient, "clean them up" so to speak, and clearly make the clinical picture clearer if not correct it.  Nosodes predate bacteriology and vaccines, but with the current modern bacteriological knowledge, we can use them to determine an accurate weapon to fight disease, and this is in line with homeopathic principles.

One more thing about these miasms is that they are not necessarily congenital or hereditary as so many physicians, even homeopaths, believe.  They are mostly acquired through skin contact, sexual intercourse or droplet infection.  The most important message to you is this:  if you suffer from a recurrent condition, and doctors have given up on you or have told you to "live with it," consider the miasms and consult a homeopathic physician.  Although the treatment of miasms is complicated a thousandfold by suppressive allopathic treatment,  miracles can happen!

The reality of these subtle, insidious miasms, which are the underlying factors in chronic disease, could be established only by a series of painstaking clinical experiments, conducted by trained and unprejudiced observers.  Imagine if Hahnemann with his keen intellect were still around and had the added advantage of knowing modern pathology.  I for one firmly believe that modern medicine would confirm most of Hahnemann's conclusions.  The facts speak for themselves: we have the testimony of hundreds of homeopaths who have applied his teachings over the last 200 years.  We also have the innumerable cures made by these physicians over these centuries.  I believe that adding modern knowledge (pathology) to Hahnemann's groundbreaking theories would provide much sought-after solutions to the cure of chronic disease. We must only hope that prejudice, greed and laziness would not interfere with this noble goal.

# CHAPTER SIX

# THE LAYER THEORY: SYMPTOMS DISAPPEAR IN REVERSE ORDER OF THEIR APPEARANCE

In my 23-year practice of medicine, one thing has always astonished me: that patients pay so little attention to the causes and effects of their diseases. What I suspect is that while many people don't want to make a connection between what they eat and how they feel (for fear they may have to "sacrifice" some of those goodies), even more people would rather not deal with the mind-body connection.

## Ignorance and Denial Obstruct Health

I have already mentioned in Chapter Four several often forgotten mental factors. Very often, to deny that they exist is to provide the basis of obstructions to the cure. It is not always lay people who fail to make the connection, a reality which is illustrated by the following example. One of my patients was a psychotherapist who was doing quite well with her indicated homeopathic remedy, until she came in my office in a foul mood, telling me that I had promised she would be all better by this time. I reviewed her clinic notes and showed her that she had been making excellent progress up to a certain point. (It is my habit to write down any significant event happening in the patient's life, even if they bring it up casually. It helped me in this case.) It was around the time of her decline that my patient --

who was going through a divorce -- heard from someone that her husband's girlfriend was expecting a child.  It was obvious to me that until that point my patient somehow had not completely made the break with her husband.   The news of the baby, because it made the breakup more irreversible, was too painful to face, so my patient stuffed it down.   When I pointed this out to her, my patient still had a hard time accepting this reality, despite her profession. She became very upset just talking about it. No other event had happened around that time, so the only aggravating trigger would have been the "hearing of bad news." By denying the impact of the news she heard, my patient only delayed her recovery and then started blaming her delay in recovery on everything else, me included.   Her anger and frustration were major blocks to recovery.

If intelligent, trained professionals can fail to see the connection, what can we expect from the average person? It is of utmost importance for every patient to become a kind of Sherlock Holmes when it comes to their own bodies. As I already mentioned, sometimes we think that we have dealt with a certain issue because our therapist has told us so.   However, by not knowing the physical signs of grief, for instance, a psychotherapist may be unable to make the proper assessment and the issue -- which should be explored further -- remains unresolved. This chapter is extremely important to patients and physicians alike:  it will be the trail to follow to get well!

## Constructing Layers Using Homeopathic Law

Homeopathy follows certain clear rules (as explained in Chapter Eight). One of these laws is Hering's Law of the Cure, named after Dr. Constantine Hering, a contemporary of Dr. Hahnemann and the founder of organized homeopathy in America. This law states, in part, that "the symptoms disappear in the reverse order of their appearance."  Imagine a patient who, after hearing bad news, falls ill with a cold and a dry cough, followed by mucus excretion.  If the treatment is correct, and the patient is on his way to a cure, we should first see the expectoration of mucus disappear, then the dry cough. Finally, the very first symptoms linked to the shock of the bad news will recur (depression, or anxiety, or whatever they were). We then know that the cure of the patient is complete without the danger of recurrence, if no more traumas happen to him. But most of the time, life is more complicated than that. Understanding the law of the cure will help the physician determine the correct therapy and will help the patient evaluate his transition to health. While being treated with the chosen homeopathic remedy, the patient must realize that the reappearance of old symptoms is a very favorable sign. It does not mean that there is an aggravation or recurrence of the disease -- it means the patient is taking the perfect road to restitution of health.

**Time-Line for Order of Treatment**

For a physician, every investigation into an illness starts with a good inquiry. Getting the facts together, the symptoms with their modalities and the different factors in the patient's lifestyle contributing to the disease are essential if we want to be successful in restoring the patient's health. Yet, most of the time, the most important question is often neglected by the physician: "What happened in your life when you became sick or just before you became sick?" I see enough doctor's reports from my patients. They are explicit enough in the description of symptoms and the enumeration of the different illnesses, but they rarely link the onset of the disease to a meaningful event in the patient's life. Yet, it is most often the clue to the solution. A pertinent example will illustrate this.

I had a young patient, 24 years old, who was diagnosed with lupus, an "incurable" autoimmune disorder. The standard treatment for lupus is cortisone and Plaquenil, in addition to various therapeutic bandaids for every other symptom from which the patient might suffer. This patient had been taking five medications, all with side-effects. Over the last three years, she had gone to the best specialists only to be told that she was going to have to live with this disease, which is progressive. To my amazement, none of these eminent practitioners had ever asked her, "What happened before you came down with the first symptoms?"

It turned out that for the five months preceding her diagnosis with lupus, this young lady had been taking care of her dying mother, to whom she was very close. One month after her mother's death, she exhibited the first symptoms of her illness. Even three years later, the prescription of an appropriate homeopathic grief remedy considerably improved all her symptoms to the extent that she could stop taking most of the allopathic drugs.   The difference between the homeopathic treatment and the Western medical treatment was that the first was aimed at the cause, the other purely at the symptoms. A miracle?  No, simply common sense, and a willingness to honor the mind-body connection.

What had happened to the young lupus patient happens to all of us to some extent.  Our lives are a succession of events, some more traumatic than others.  A human being is like an onion, wrapped in many different layers.  Each time a person is subjected to a physical or emotional injury, strong enough to create symptoms, we have a new layer to treat.  A person suffering with a chronic ailment usually has a long medical story encompassing a number of ailments which have been manifested at different periods in the patient's life.  To the homeopath, the entire history is a connected sequence of different initiating causes.  In order to accomplish a real "cure," it is necessary not only to eliminate the ailment from which the patient is currently complaining, but also the entire background of disease. This means that a well-chosen homeopathic remedy will have the result of regressing the patient (though often in a less aggravated form), through every illness that has been suffered in his or her life. This is mainly because all those previous illnesses were suppressed, not cured. Frequently a series of different remedies is required, given one at a time, according to the symptoms presented by the patient.   As mentioned in the previous law of Hering, when the symptoms of past complaints reappear in reverse order, this indicates to the homeopathic physician that he (or she) is on the right track towards a genuine condition of good health.

This is completely different from what we do in modern medicine.   Ask a so-called "mainstream" physician what constitutes a cure, and he is apt to say that the results of the disease must be removed. If there is a tumor, cut it out. If there is an abscess, drain it. If digestion is disordered and intestines clogged, use a purge. If there is fever, use a medicine to lower the temperature. Sounds easy, doesn't it? But are such treatments real and complete? Far from it. This attempt to treat disease solely on the basis of tissue changes ignores the person who lives in his or her body as a house. Such treatment removes external expressions of disorder without curing the disorder itself, and so sends the expression deeper into more vital centers, the organs. It will make the patient incurable and is partly responsible for the increase in nervous disorders, cancers, TB and mental disease. "The ideal cure" on the other hand, will follow the homeopathic laws as explained in Chapter Eight.

A hypothetical case will illustrate the homeopathic view of chronic disease with its different layers. A 35-year-old female is suffering from an array of chronic symptoms: fatigue, brainfag, sensitivities to food and environment, recurrent colds and flus, change in disposition from irritability to depression, PMS, irregular menstrual cycles and periods of vertigo. In other words, a classic presentation of a CFIDS patient. Her time-line reveals the following events:

• Age 3 to 10: grew up in an abusive family, with dominant, alcoholic father; was withdrawn, timid, often left alone by herself after school since both parents worked. Had recurrent ear infections and sore throats from age 3 on;

• Age 12: onset of puberty, first menstrual cycle; had acne, which was aggravated before each menstrual cycle, and for which tetracycline was prescribed; health declined, with more frequent illnesses, keeping her out of school;

• Age 21 to 32: was married to a verbally abusive husband; experienced increased weakness, and for the first time, sensitivities towards food and environment; divorced at age 31, after which she felt relief;

• Age 34: was involved in a car accident, and experienced severe whiplash; had definite aggravation of the existing symptoms and appearance of new symptoms such as headaches and neck stiffness.

When we analyze this time-line, we can definitely see the different layers which produced this woman's symptoms. The last and outermost layer, the car accident, was intense enough to produce new symptoms, as well as aggravate existing symptoms. This is called the "trauma" layer. The chosen remedy has to be a trauma remedy, such as Arnica, for instance. If this remedy is the right one, the new symptoms related to the accident (which were the last symptoms to appear), will disappear first.

The second layer is what we can call an "abusive" layer. Through the long-standing abusive mistreatment, the patient's dignity was taken away. Typically, we will see a depressed patient, who wilts under confrontation, has little self-confidence, exhibits recurrent bladder infections and vaginism or pain with intercourse. To dissolve this layer, another remedy, for instance Staphysagria, will be needed. The physician can expect that this remedy will be given over a longer period of time, since this layer was built up over a period of 11 years. It is not unusual, at this point, that by regressing into this layer, old emotional symptoms and even "old" physical symptoms, such as bladder infections, will come back. Again, it is important not to misinterpret the reappearance of these old symptoms -- the patient's situation is not aggravating, but improving!

The third layer is definitely hormonally related, with the appearance of acne that was aggravated around the menstrual cycle. Intake of tetracycline might have also aggravated the situation. The physician may often take the patient's history again at this point, since the patient is presenting with the old symptom, as the patient experienced them around puberty. A new remedy again will be prescribed according to all the symptoms and their etiology.

The final layer is the layer of abandonment, loneliness and grief this patient experienced as a young child. Obviously, this trauma was intense enough to undermine her immune system and cause recurrent colds. Again, the homeopathic physician has at his disposition at least 50 remedies. He will choose the one that fits the whole person presented before him.

As you can see, with the help of an experienced homeopath, you can dissolve the different layers that have come from the traumas in your life. The process is relatively fast, smooth and gentle. The patient can help the physician enormously by bringing along to the first office visit a time-line explaining the different physical and emotional factors which had a great impact on the person. However, it is important to be wary: we don't all react in the same way to the same triggering factor. For some, the breakup of a relationship can be heartbreaking. For others it is a relief. In the latter case, no aggravation of symptoms will occur, as no layer has been created and no remedy will be needed to dissolve it.

This section on the causes of disease would not be complete if I didn't mention the two other important factors: diet and what the Chinese called external factors. The diet section is discussed in Chapter 12. For more in-depth information on the diet, also refer to my books, <u>Full of Life</u> and <u>How to Dine Like the Devil, and Feel Like a Saint.</u> My book, <u>Full of Life</u>, also discusses the external factors in detail. But it is the mental factors and the hereditary factors that determine the existence of chronic disease in a human being.

## When "Like Cures Like"

Before closing this chapter, I want to talk about a type of case that is fairly common in homeopathic practice, in which the curative remedy turns out to be one to which the patient was exposed in the first place. There is reason to believe that the presenting illness represents, in effect, the proving of the remedy in a person abnormally sensitive to it. In other words, the patient was exposed to a minimal quantity of an "exterior" factor, but his increased sensitivity to the substance was the cause of his illness. These cases are very useful prototypes in studying and treating a wide range of illnesses attributable to environmental and industrial poisons. Some examples will clarify this.

One of the most spectacular recoveries I observed was in a 37-year-old man who was diagnosed with CFIDS 15 years before I saw him. Since his original diagnosis, his situation had progressively worsened, and various therapies had been unsuccessful at alleviating even his most severe symptoms. When he described his symptoms to me, he painted for me the perfect picture of Arsenic. When I mentioned this to him, he stared at  me in disbelief.  He happened to be a chemist by profession, and at the time he became sick, he had been working with arsenic.  Of  course, lab tests performed at that time turned out to be negative for arsenic poisoning but that only confirms the insensitivity of our lab tests when it comes to detecting trace amounts of a substance in the body's bloodstream.

When I prescribed Arsenicum album (the homeopathic arsenic), he improved dramatically within three weeks (and this after a 15-year story of CFIDS symptoms).  This should be a warning to those physicians pursuing the elusive "virus" in the etiology of CFIDS!

Another case was that of a 30-year-old man who had been suffering for six years with an itchy, crusty seborrhea of the scalp. He also suffered from lower back pains, which were worse upon awakening (experienced as stiffness, but which improved with movement).  After an initial therapy with a well-indicated remedy was unsuccessful, he then told me that he had always been very sensitive to poison ivy.  Homeopathic poison ivy, or Rhus toxicodendron, gave him prompt and lasting relief.

In the above mentioned cases, there was prior contact with the offending substance.  The present illness was consistent with the proving or clinical picture of the substance; and the same substance in homeopathic dose proved effective and curative as a remedy.  In both cases, the connection had to be elicited by careful questioning and was totally unsuspected by the patient. But it showed the beauty of the first homeopathic law, *like cures like*.

All this should lead us to wonder whether a great many of our common diseases such as arthritis and cancer are not originating from single or repetitive exposure to poisonous substances.  The distinction between remedies and poisons, and therefore between cure and poisoning, is essentially one of dosage and individual sensitivity.  Many of our greatest homeopathic remedies (arsenic, the snake venoms, hemlock, etc.), are poisons in their crude and undiluted states.  Certainly, it is no secret that the process of industrialization has itself threatened the existence of life on this planet, partly by bringing a number of highly toxic substances into common use, and also by recklessly using up all the natural resources.

I'll leave you with another interesting case, which I recently read about. A 60-year-old man suffered from "chronic ulcerative colitis." He also suffered from severe itching and his whole body was covered with ulcerating skin lesions, diagnosed as "neurodermatitis." The whole case resolved quickly when his wife happened to mention that his itching was worse in the evening from 8 p.m. to 10 p.m. Only one remedy in our homeopathic repertoire has this symptom: Kreosotum. When this was mentioned, the cause was found for his entire clinical condition. Over the last ten years, as a hobby he had stained all the woodwork in his house with a mixture of creosote and crankcase oil, exposing himself to this chemical. A single dose of homeopathic creosote relieved all his symptoms.

As you can see, the remedy in all of the above cases was not just given because there was exposure to the substance. The patients also showed the proven clinical symptoms of those remedies. This suggests that there is no easy method of recognizing these cases; the best that can be done is to be aware of the possibility. The homeopathic physician, through painstakingly taking the patient's full personal and medical history, has a much better chance of recognizing the connection between toxic substances and the appearance of illness than his Western-trained counterpart.

# SECTION THREE

## HOMEOPATHY:

## "TAKE A LITTLE ARSENIC AND FEEL BETTER IN THE MORNING!"

# CHAPTER SEVEN

## HISTORY OF A SCIENTIFIC MEDICINE

Homeopathy is so intimately associated with the name of Hahnemann that we would be remiss not to try to get to know him better. Alas! We know about the saying, "A hero is not appreciated till he passes away." It was certainly no different with our master of homeopathy. Evoke the name of Samuel Hahnemann, M.D., and you will draw a blank from most modern orthodox physicians. The very few who make the connection to his masterful art of homeopathy will either admire him or reject him according to the efforts they have made to study the subject.

Born April 11, 1755 in a small East German town, Hahnemann came from a poor family that could barely pay for his education. In spite of being physically weak, he showed an exceptional talent for study. By the age of 12, he was employed to teach others Greek and Latin. His rule in studying was to "read little, but correctly," and then "to digest what he had read," which shows us how he would do one thing at a time, and do it thoroughly. This was Hahnemann's trademark: he never published a book before he had explored his theories for many years through careful, painstaking work.

At the age of 20, Hahnemann began his studies of medicine, earning his way by translating foreign medical books. At the age of 24 he passed his examination for a medical degree and two years later he married a pharmacist's daughter who was to be his companion for 47 years and bear him 11 children. While he was practicing as a general physician, he took a rather dim view of the medical practice in general and his own practice of medicine in particular. He candidly admitted that most of his patients would have done better had he let them alone. It was the time of blood-letting with leeches, the use of emetics, purgatives, and agents provoking perspiration and urination. These treatments were used "under the delusion" said Hahnemann, "of being able to weaken and eradicate the imagined disease substance...but by these very means, they increased the patient's suffering."

If it weren't so sad it would have looked almost comical: patients suffering from high fevers or other restless syndromes, weakened by their doctor's treatments; family members thanking them for their "good deeds." Indeed, all they saw was that the previously struggling and restless patient was, all of a sudden, very calm and immobile. Little did they know that this was only due to the acts of those same physicians, that weakened the patients to the extent that most of them suffered a hastened death.

No wonder Hahnemann, who was much too honest and human, retired with disgust from the medical profession and devoted himself to chemistry and literature. In 1789, he wrote his first book, *On Syphilis*. The most remarkable fact in that book is his discovery of a "new" preparation: soluble mercury as a therapy for syphilis. It is still being used today as a remarkable homeopathic remedy and bears the name of Mercurius solibilis Hahnemanian.

The biggest turning point of his life came in 1790, when he was translating Cullen's *Materia Medica* and discovered the fever-producing properties of cinchona bark, from a tree indigenous to Peru. This was to Hahnemann what the falling apple was to Newton's concept of physics: the birth of a new concept of medicine. Hahnemann selflessly performed original testing with cinchona on himself. His conclusion: "Peruvian bark, which is used as a remedy for intermittent fevers, acts because it can produce symptoms similar to those of intermittent fever in healthy people." With these words, a new law of healing was born: *"Similia similibus curentur"* or *"Like cures like."*

In 1796, Hahnemann wrote the remarkable *Essay on a New Principle for Ascertaining the Remedial Powers of Medicinal Substances*, in which he expressed the above law. But due to the jealousy of his colleagues, and contrary to the law and common sense, Hahnemann was prohibited from dispensing his own medicines. Even after he was successful in 1799 in eradicating a severe epidemic of scarlet fever with Belladonna, the continued hostility and jealousy of his fellow physicians drove him from his home town.

The next years he wandered with his family from one place to another, in deep poverty, still writing many articles, denouncing the absurdity of ordinary medical practice. Finally, in 1810, he published the first edition of his immortal *Organon*. In spite of further attacks from the so-called great medical minds of his time, Hahnemann pursued his course, answering all attacks on his person with silent contempt. In 1811, he published the first volume of the *Pure Materia Medica*, which contained the homeopathic pictures of all the remedies he had been silently testing on himself and friends. It has to be stressed that all criticism aimed towards Hahnemann by the medical establishment was based entirely on theoretical and personal grounds. No attempt was made by those "honorable" physicians to put the system to the test of bedside experience.

Finding little support among the German medical profession, Hahnemann moved to Leipzig where he began to lecture on homeopathy. In addition to careful prescribing, Hahnemann attached much importance to the total health maintenance of his patients. He would go into the smallest details as what to eat and drink, how much air and exercise to take, and when to take cold and warm baths. Quite an improvement over the barbaric methods of his contemporaries, who locked their patients up in warm, stuffy rooms without fresh air, and put the "insane" or mentally disturbed (the deaf was one such category) in mental asylums where they died a cruel death. Hahnemann was indeed the first to practice public health in history; and even in his masterwork, the *Organon*, he never fails to mention the subject of diet.

Hahnemann's last great work was published in 1928: a book on his theory of miasms, *Chronic Diseases.* It was a difficult book and it divided many of his followers who claimed that Hahnemann was getting senile. At the age of 80, he was married for the second time to a young French woman, Melanie, who convinced him to move to Paris. There he found the atmosphere he was looking for, and in fact, it was there that he finished what was to be his greatest gift to mankind, the sixth edition of the <u>Organon</u>. Doctors attested to the fact that Hahnemann was of sound mind and geniality until the last days of his life. He was 88 when he died. He was the only human being who had in his own lifespan discovered and finished the totality of a science. Long before Pasteur and Koch, Hahnemann mentioned "small, invisible" organisms responsible for disease. Therefore, Hahnemann could also be called one of the fathers of microbiology! Even more important, he was the only physician of his time who treated and wiped out epidemics of scarlet fever, typhoid fever and cholera. This man was truly ahead of his time. Why then isn't homeopathy universally accepted today? The next portion of the chapter will explore the reasons for homeopathy's decline.

## Decline of Homeopathy

At the beginning of this century, homeopathy was flourishing in Europe and the United States. There were numerous homeopathic medical schools, hospitals and practicing physicians. Looking at the enormous success homeopathy had in the treatment of epidemics, it seems almost inconceivable that this prominent science could be pushed into the background. Yet it was. How did this happen?

One factor was the discovery of modern medications and the notion of the "quick fix." The first so-called "magic bullet" was discovered by Paul Ehrlich in 1909: salvarsan, an anti-bacterial drug. Sir Alexander Fleming discovered penicillin in 1928 and fueled the belief that every possible human disease was within a breath of being conquered. At the time, physicians were dazzled by the apparent phenomenal "cures" of these wonder drugs and turned away from homeopathy, the less spectacular and much more difficult to grasp science. Physicians now are no different. After studying many different kinds of medicine, I can assure you that homeopathy is by far the most difficult to learn, discouraging young physicians who would rather stick to their prescription pads in order to effect a "cure. " Of course, once pharmaceutical companies found out how much more money there was to make from these new medications, millions of dollars were poured into research and advertisement to hail the miracles of modern medicine. We physicians know that this is essentially unchanged today.

The homeopaths did not help their own case either. Even now, it is difficult for the patient to distinguish between different homeopathic practitioners who all claim that they are practicing "classical" homeopathy. The real cause of this is that the sixth and last edition of the *Organon*, the bible of homeopathy, was not released until 1923. Melanie Hahnemann, Samuel's widow, resisted releasing the newly finished manuscript which Hahnemann claimed was his "best one yet to come." Was it greed (reportedly she asked $50,000, an enormous sum in that time) or overprotectiveness and control (she claimed that the world was not ready yet to receive the latest work of the master)? The question is still unanswered. But the result was and still is devastating: most homeopaths (about 90%) even today still practice according to the 5th edition of the *Organon* (also called the Kentian method, named after the enormously popular American, Chicago-based physician James Tyler Kent).

But in the 6th edition, Hahnemann stated unequivocally "to forget everything he wrote in the 5th edition," comparing those methods employed in the 5th edition to barbarism, since the high-dose therapy (See Chapter Nine) often leads to serious homeopathic aggravation. This is analogous to following all the facts we knew about neurology in 1952 and refusing to practice according to what we know today in 1992. The reader should keep in mind that there is this rift and that you may want to read Chapter Nine before consulting a practitioner, so you know the correct questions to ask. At any rate, one can imagine that the division among homeopaths does not lead to strength in the profession.

## Homeopathy's Comeback

In spite of the "magical" successes of modern medicine and the in-fighting among homeopaths, homeopathy has made a resounding comeback since 1960. There are several reasons for this. First of all, there is increased concern about the side-effects of modern medicines. It is hard to imagine any medication that does not have a serious side effect, which often leads to the prescription of more medications. It is like a domino effect. I see elderly patients in my office who take ten medications at a time: five for organic lesions or symptoms they have, the other five to counter the side-effects of the first five medications. Those side-effects do not always show up immediately. In spite of "infallible" double-blind studies, every year medications are taken off the market because of serious side-effects, even deaths, that they cause. But pharmaceutical companies, afraid to lose billions of dollars in income, fight with all their influence any removal of medications, persecuting anyone who blows the whistle.

You also can imagine the increased cost this over-prescribing puts on the health system of any country. It breaks my heart to read in the newspapers that poor families cannot go to the doctor because they can't afford the expensive medication. Yet most of the pediatric problems in American could be treated for the nominal sum of <u>one cent per month!</u>

Do I need to bring up the countless victims of addiction to modern medicines? Forgetting what an immense treasure we have in homeopathic remedies to treat emotional and mental disease, physicians have bombarded the public with powerful, addictive tranquilizers, which, again, do not cure, but suppress and create much greater illnesses than the ones they were intended to treat. What a tragedy it is to know that more people die from over-medication each year than from car accidents.

As if nature itself wants to show the limits of modern medicine, old epidemics have made a resurgence, and new ones have taken hold, defying the effectiveness of the present medicines (See Chapter 10). Tuberculosis again has the public health departments across the country scared because of new strains resistant to antibiotics. Gonorrhea and syphilis are rampant and also elude modern antibiotics. Then we have the rise of diseases, many resulting from the hazards of lifestyle: AIDS, hepatitis, heart disease and cancer are increasing at alarming rates.

Another factor that I see, and in which I take pride and joy, is that patients are becoming more intelligent and want to take more of an active part in their own healing. In spite of whatever is presented to them, patients are recognizing that many modern therapeutic interventions are only bringing temporary relief and not really leading to the path of health as explained in Chapter One. The task of the modern physician is to be a healer and an educator. Only his own continuous unbiased studying will allow him to do this. Let's turn to homeopathy and consider its advantages.

### Advantages of Homeopathy

1. The treatment is individualized -- it considers the whole patient himself <u>through</u> symptoms, rather than the disease as a name. The previous Chapter on "Causes of Disease" stressed the different ideological factors which could lead to a similar clinical picture. Do we treat two patients with CFIDS exactly alike if one became ill after taking "the pill," and the other after a marital breakup? In Western medicine, yes! In homeopathy, no!

Too often, we physicians think that our work is finished when we put the patient in a category of disease. "Yes, you have chronic fatigue. Go home and rest and pray that it will go away." Or, "You have an unidentified viral disease," the catch-all category of modern disease which really translates into, "I don't know what you have but rather than losing face, I want to use some medical jargon to get me off the hook." Homeopathy does not even need a name of disease. It looks at the person as a whole and tries to find the contributing factors of disease.

2. All drugs recommended in homeopathy have had <u>extensive human experiment</u>. Contrary to what opponents of homeopathy would have you believe, all remedies are tested in the **only** scientific way, i.e. on normal, healthy human beings, not lab animals. Besides the cruelty done to animals, I could never understand why lab results in animals could be trusted to give the same results in human beings. Hahnemann and his early supporters did the only thing a physician should do when recommending a new treatment: they tested it on themselves.

3. The homeopathic method of prescribing on a totality of symptoms is designed to be curative, not just palliative and suppressive as when one takes a sleeping pill for insomnia. It bears repeating: little in Western medicine is directed at reparation. Most symptoms get suppressed, leading to the false belief that the disease is cured, when in reality the patient is continuing on his path of disease.

4. Just as with Chinese medicine, homeopathy has its time-tested usefulness. No method of medical treatment can last almost 200 years in all climates, races and ages, and not be founded on natural laws. Medical fads run their course and disappear rapidly, whereas homeopathy is practiced all over the world and survives in spite of negative public reaction by unscrupulous, uninformed people.

5. There is no drugging effect, and there are no side-effects from homeopathic remedies. That does not mean that there cannot be unwanted effects. But a truly well-trained homeopath recognizes what a homeopathic aggravation is (See Chapter Nine). In order not to fall into the pitfalls of modern medicine, it is therefore imperative that whoever claims to practice homeopathy is properly trained. Sounds logical to you and me, but this is not always the case. Homeopathy, even more than acupuncture, requires extensive training. Professionals practicing homeopathy without sufficient knowledge do a great disservice to their patients and to homeopathy in general.

6. Its cost is modest and its application is simple. Once you discover how to put your remedy in water (See Chapter Nine), you will be truly amazed at the astonishing low cost of homeopathy. Everyone should have a home-kit with about twenty remedies and be familiar with the remedies. In acute situations, especially with children, the miracle of homeopathy will truly unfold before your eyes. The application and dosages are very simple. Either a little lactose or cane sugar-coated pellets melt immediately on the tongue, or the remedy is taken in water and a few teaspoons a day suffice. There are no painful shots, no unpleasant taste, and no unpleasant, immediate side-effects.

7. Most of the remedies are prepared from fresh plants or minerals. Properly stored in a regular cupboard away from heat or radiation, they keep their strength indefinitely. Compare that with the deterioration of most medications after some years.

Isn't it amazing that despite this long list of the benefits of homeopathy that some not-so-well-intentioned people still label this great science as quackery? I am inviting those critics to read on to the next paragraph and see just how modern medicine has heavily borrowed from homeopathy.

## Unrecognized Use of Homeopathy in Conventional Medicine

It might be quite a revelation to those hard-nosed critics to realize that homeopathy is used unwittingly by orthodox doctors in the midst of their allopathic prescribing. But, they did not listen to Hahnemann who said, *"Imitate me, but imitate me well."* The result is that all these remedies without side-effects became medications **with** side-effects. Let us look at the different medications that were borrowed from homeopathy. I have to emphasize here that it is not the <u>dosage</u> of a remedy that makes it homeopathic but the similarity of the provings to the symptoms of the patient.

First of all there is the first homeopathic remedy ever proven by Hahnemann, *Cinchona* or the Peruvian bark. Its use (known as Quinine) in malaria and heart rhythm disorders is well-known. Then there is *Colchicine*. Preparations of the autumn crocus, as it is known, have been used in orthodox medicine to fight acute gout. *Digitalis* for heart failure is used in heart failure but in Western doses causes at least 60,000 deaths a year. The use of *Argentum Nitricum* can be evidenced in ophthalmia neonatorum -- silver nitrate drops that are put into the eyes of newborns -- a common practice to avoid damage from gonorrhea infection.

One of the most common examples of homeopathic prescribing in conventional medicine is the use of *sulphur* and sulfur-containing drugs. Sulfur is of great value in the treatment of various skin eruptions: acne, seborrheic dermatitis, psoriasis and rosacea. A quick look in my dermatology book shows me all the different uses of 3% to 10% sulfur lotions in the above mentioned skin diseases. Among the provings of sulfur are diarrhea with mucus and blood. The use of sulphasalazine in colitis ulcerosa may well be a homeopathic action.

We use *Selenium* conventionally for scalp seborrhea. It is interesting to note for us homeopaths that Selenium homeopathically has itching eruptions of the scalp with hair fallout. *Fluoric acid* and *calcium fluoride* in toxic doses cause defects in tooth enamel and result in rapid caries (cavities). Yet, we all know of the controversial addition of fluoride in our drinking water, aimed to protect teeth against dental caries. In cases of arthritis, modern medicine often uses gold injections to alleviate the inflammation and pain. Often, therapy is halted because of serious side effects, especially in sensitive patients. It is too bad that modern medicine cannot make the connection with the homeopathic remedy *Aurum Metallicum* or the metal gold. It has in its clinical picture many arthritic symptoms with swollen, painful joints. This gold, applied according to homeopathic principles instead of randomly as is done in modern use, would avoid serious side-effects and would be more individually indicated, cutting down on failures considerably. We all know of *Ipecac* used in conventional medicine as an emetic or vomit-inducing substance in the treatment of poisoning.

There are still more examples, too many to mention here. The main point is that there are many people today with chronic illnesses of all kinds, maintained on expensive, toxic drugs, and yet not cured. Not cured because the root of their symptoms has not been rectified with the appropriate drug. Too many patients are suffering from iatrogenic or doctor-induced [also treatment induced] illness (35% of all the diseases according to the World Health Organization (WHO)!). Although the homeopathic practitioner might not be able to cure all of them, he will treat the patient as a whole person, as an individual prescribing affordable medicines without side-effects. I hope that modern medicine, having borrowed heavily from the vegetable and mineral kingdoms, will use them wisely, and in the words of Hahnemann, *"restore the sick to health which is our highest and only mission."*

# CHAPTER EIGHT

## HOMEOPATHY:
## HOW DOES IT WORK?

*"As this natural law of curing manifests itself in any absolute experiment and in any true experience of this world and, consequently must be acknowledged as a fact; the scientific explanation how it be possible, is of little importance and I do not set a high value on making any attempt at something of that sort"*

*--- Samuel Hahnemann, M.D.*

In June 1988, an article written by the French researcher Dr. Jacques Benveniste appeared in the respectable science magazine <u>Nature</u>, and unleashed a storm of controversy.[1] The bottom line of Benveniste's finding was that "it is possible to dilute a watery solution of an antibody indefinitely <u>without the solution losing its biological activity</u>." There was no objective explanation for this. But Benveniste kept an open mind and on many occasions, he responded to referees' suggestions at great inconvenience to himself. When told, for example, that the experiments should be repeated at an independent laboratory, he arranged for this to be done. The experiments were subsequently repeated <u>with exactly the same results.</u> The same experiments were repeated at universities in Israel, Italy and Canada, with the exact same results.

---

1. *"Human basophil degranulation triggered by very dilute antiserum against IgE',* Davenas, Benveniste; INSERM U200, Universite de Paris; *Nature* Vol. 333; 30 June, 1988.

But did science hail this as a breakthrough? No. Benveniste's findings were rejected.

The backlash was enormous. <u>Nature</u> sent out a "professional" team to disprove Benveniste's findings. But who were these "professionals?" A professional magician, a journalist, and a statistician. Benveniste allowed them to see his experiments, which speaks for his integrity. But how would mainstream doctors react to the same team sent to scrutinize their latest findings on, say, Alzheimer research? I think they probably would not be as gracious as Benveniste was.

These "highly-qualified" investigators were also "dismayed" to learn that the salaries of two co-authors of the published article were paid by Boiron, a supplier of homeopathic pharmaceuticals. In light of their investigations, they believed that such use amounted to "misuse." Following the same principles, we might as well throw <u>most</u> of the Western medical research out because <u>the majority of its experiments are paid for by pharmaceutical companies.</u> Unfortunately for science, and homeopathy in particular, a result that challenged fundamental science was thrown out and with it, a chance of discovering exciting new laws in medicine.

## Common-Sense Principles of Homeopathy

While homeopathy continues to be the step-child of medicine in the Western world, there are nevertheless proven principles on which it is built. The remainder of this chapter will cover those seven principles or pillars upon which homeopathy rests, according to Dr. Pierre Schmidt, an eminent Swiss homeopathic physician.

1. **The law of like to cure like**
2. **The use of a single remedy according to the similarity**
3. **Experimentation on healthy individuals**
4. **The infinitesimal dose**
5. **Individualization**
6. **The rules for applying remedies**
7. **The theory of the miasms**

Although almost 200 years old, these laws are still valid today. These rules act as a guide to the well-trained practitioner, who practices them as effective and risk-free remedies. Established medicine, on the other hand, is still looking for an approach that deals with man as a whole, not parts. Let's review these different pillars of homeopathy.

## 1. The law of like cures like

This was not necessarily Hahnemann's brainchild. Hippocrates himself understood that a sick person cannot be considered apart from his environment and that illness is a condition of the whole patient. Hahnemann, being the keen observer that he was, looked on with horror at what his fellow physicians were practicing according to their law, "The contrary cures the contrary." In his 6th edition of the *Organon, Par. 59* he writes:

*"Important symptoms of persistent diseases have never yet been treated with such palliative antagonistic remedies, without a relapse -- indeed, a palpable aggravation of the malady, occurring a few hours later... For nocturnal coughs of long standing the ordinary physician knew no better than to administer opium, whose primary action is to suppress every irritation; the cough would then perhaps cease the first night, but during the subsequent nights it would be still more severe, and if it were again suppressed, fever and nocturnal perspiration were added to the disease. . . How often in one word, the disease is aggravated by the secondary action of such antagonistic remedies, the old school with its false theories does not perceive but experience teaches it in a terrible manner. If these ill-effects are produced, the ordinary physician imagines he can get over the difficulty by giving, at each renewed aggravation, a stronger dose of the remedy. . ."*

These wise words were written 200 years ago, yet modern medicine still makes those mistakes of the "old-school physician." Often, the physician will give a suppressive cough syrup followed by antibiotics for simple viral infections. When they don't work, they choose yet another stronger antibiotic, only to confirm that not much has changed since the follies of doctors in Hahnemann's time.

In Paragraph 61, he writes,

*"Had physicians been capable of reflecting on the sad results of the antagonistic employment of medicines, they had long since discovered the grand truth, THAT THE TRUE RADICAL HEALING ART MUST BE FOUND IN THE EXACT OPPOSITE OF SUCH AN ANTIPATHIC TREATMENT OF THE SYMPTOMS OF DISEASE. ."* (capital letters added for emphasis by author)

Hahnemann came by this conclusion from first-hand experience. At age 35, while translating a medical book, he was struck by the conflicting reports about quinine. He decided, as a true and inquiring physician, to try it on himself. After several days of administration, he began to experience the fever symptoms similar to those for which quinine was the remedy. Soon after, he experimented with other substances and came to the same conclusion: a substance can cure what it induces, or like can cure like.

### 2. The use of a single remedy

When the physician decides upon a homeopathic remedy according to the totality of the symptoms (i.e., taking the whole person with his emotions and physical symptoms into account), he will prescribe ONE remedy at a time. By administering this remedy by itself, the practitioner will be able to distinguish its actions from the interfering effects of other substances. Patients should not take "mixed" preparations of homeopathics, so common on the market in tincture form. Practitioners using these mixtures do so out of laziness -- they are not willing to spend the necessary years studying -- and prefer to prescribe mixtures with esoteric names such as "grief" or "abandonment."

Hahnemann would have had nothing but contempt for these practitioners, who have the audacity to call themselves "classical" homeopaths. Hahnemann himself said, *"it is impossible from any knowledge we possess of the separate actions of remedies, to predict what will be their effects in combination."*

As you can see, the mixing of homeopathic medicines is not only contrary to the fundamental idea of homeopathy, but it does not allow us *a posteriori* to obtain knowledge about the actions of our medicines. If pharmaceutical companies want to develop mixtures, they should do so according to the principles of homeopathy and test their pure effects on healthy individuals (provings).   Otherwise, the mixture-practice is a dangerous innovation, because we don't have the slightest evidence to show that the action of a chemical compound will be at all similar to that of both the simple substances of which it is composed.  To demonstrate my point even further, in Paragraph 273 of the *Organon*, Hahnemann says,

*"In no case under treatment is it necessary and therefore not permissible to administer to a patient more than one single, simple medicinal substance at one time.   It is absolutely not allowed in homeopathy, the one true, simple and natural art of healing, to give the patient at one time two different medicinal substances. . ."*

### 3. Experimentation on healthy individuals

From ancient times until well into the 18th century, much of what was known about drugs was based on pure speculation. In 1666, a dean of the Paris Faculty of Medicine, Dr. Patin, wrote:

*"They say that poison is not a poison in the hands of a good doctor.  Most of them have killed their wives, their children, or their friends, and yet notwithstanding they go on to speak of a drug they themselves would not dare to touch."*

It would be helpful even in our times, where many experimental drugs and vaccinations are tried on desperate patients, for doctors to try them on themselves first. This is where Hahnemann's approach was revolutionary.  For the first time in the history of medicine, a doctor conceived the idea of testing medicines on himself.   And later, under his supervision, his pupils, all doctors, experimented with a vast number of substances, notating all the effects. Before Hahnemann did this, the effects of drugs were only known as a result of accidental poisonings.

Modern medicine carries out its experiments on animals and thereafter the drugs are tested exclusively on ill individuals. For opponents to say that homeopathy is not based on any scientific basis is therefore completely unfounded, as it is tested in the only sound scientific way: on healthy human beings. This was called **provings** of the remedy. To prove one single remedy, many provers will do the testing as no single person feels all the symptoms which a remedy can produce in the human organism. Each subject will only feel a certain number of these symptoms. This also means that when your physician chooses a remedy, and you read about the remedy in the *Materia Medica,* that you can't say that the remedy is not good for you until you try it -- everyone shows different symptoms of the same remedy. This is what we call positive and negative matching.

### 4. The infinitesimal dose

Whenever Hahnemann did provings, he deliberately took a rather high dose of the remedy for consecutive days. This would give rise to authentic medical illness. But Hahnemann's version of the "high dose" pales in comparison with the dosages prescribed by modern physicians. These dosages produce an "over-effect" (a euphemism for side effects) at the patient's expense. Hahnemann understood perfectly well that heavy doses of a remedy would add unnecessary strain to the patient's body, which was already supporting its sickness.

When a drug is administered in large dosages, three types of effects occur:

a) <u>A physiological effect,</u> a direct organic reflex reaction to the drug. It is this effect that allopathic physicians look for.

b) <u>Toxic effects,</u> since often the physiological dose is not far below the toxic dose. Add to this the different degree of the patient's sensitivity; that what is physiological to

one patient is toxic for the next one; and that even the
same person will not always need the same dose at every
moment of the day.  But you and I don't have a safety
system built in to avoid "overflow" of the drug.
c) <u>Subtle effects</u> on the feelings of the patients. These are
of no interest to the allopath but are of prime interest to
the homeopath.  As explained in Chapter One, correct
therapy has to lead to a sense of well-being.

In order to obtain strong physiological responses from
their drugs, allopaths often increase the dosage of medications,
producing uncomfortable and unnatural reactions.  If you are
going to take several courses of antibiotics to fight a common
cold, this gross misuse of dosages often results in toxic symptoms
(diarrhea through destruction of the normal flora) and a clogging
of the body with drug residue.  None of this happens when the
same drugs are administered in highly diluted or homeopathic
form: there are no toxic effects and since the amount of
therapeutic substance is minimal, no residue is left in the body.
And of course, the clinical effects are better, as is so well
demonstrated by the 200 years of clinical research begun by
Hahnemann.

Can you see what possibilities this opens up? Taxol, a
drug derived from the yew tree, was approved for treatment of
breast cancer and ovarian cancer in December, 1992.  But we need
to cut down thousands and thousands of these trees to benefit a
few patients.  Precisely, four trees are needed for the dose of taxol
for one person.  The result is: toxic effects, high prices and
disruption of nature. Isn't it sad to think that we could do the
same thing with the bark of ONE tree, make a homeopathic
remedy from it and have a source of taxol for the rest of the
world, <u>for generations to come!</u>  This is true because with
homeopathic remedies we can keep on grafting the original
remedy to produce the unlimited stock.  The results would be
lower prices, no toxic drug residue, and saving our planet from
destruction -- not to mention, most likely better clinical results.

It was Hahnemann's human qualities that forced him to
look for lower and lower doses of drugs.  Paragraph 2 of the
*Organon* reads:

*"The highest ideal of cure is rapid, <u>gentle</u> and permanent restoration of health, or removal and annihilation of the disease in this whole extent, in the shortest, most reliable, and most <u>harmless way,</u> on easily comprehensive principles."*

By attenuating the dosage of the remedy, Hahnemann was able to observe that the effects of the remedy, far from diminishing, became still more powerful. Benveniste, as mentioned at the opening of the chapter, showed this precise effect with modern technology. But the medical and scientific worlds would have had to rethink their whole philosophy if they had accepted his research. For too many people, it's too scary to think that what you have been doing most of your life was based on incomplete or wrong principles.

### 5. Individualization

In this aspect, homeopathy again differs so much from Western medicine, where every CFIDS patient is treated with the same medications, and every arthritis patient receives the same treatment regimen. Because his medical theories are based on pathology, the modern physician is pleased when he can put the patient in a category. That box contains a certain amount of medications, and when used up, the patient "has to live" with his illness or has to wait until the discovery of the next drug that will land in that box.

As we have already abundantly shown, homeopathy views the patient as a whole, without having to put him in a category. The homeopathic physician is interested in every symptom of the patient: mental, emotional and physical. A homeopathic prescription is made based on the <u>totality of the symptoms</u>. However, this does not mean that all symptoms have the same importance. Hahnemann expresses again the importance of finding the remedy for those symptoms "which are most striking, most uncommon, most personal and particular."

It is amazing to think that these uncommon symptoms are not understood and have no value to the allopathic physician. Tell him that you have a metallic taste in the mouth, that you are very sensitive to the sun, that you have a restless mind with restless legs, that you can't stand to have tight clothes on, that your hair turns prematurely gray, and you a draw a blank stare from your physician or he will wave the information away, claiming it has no importance. Or, he will say, "let's take each of those symptoms one by one and prescribe multiple drugs to cover the disease picture."

Yet, for the homeopathic physician, it will be the clue for the selection of his remedy. Besides the most peculiar symptoms, homeopaths pay much attention to the mental symptoms which most reveal the personality of a patient. While it is normal that a patient would feel reticent to talk about these deepest feelings on the first consultation, much is obtained from pure observation. The trained practitioner will note the way patients greet him, and the way they start talking. Some patients can't stop talking, while others have to be prompted for one-word answers. Some patients cry while they tell their stories; others remain passionless and stoic, even while telling of intimate, horrible events. The homeopathic physician will observe and take notes: certain gestures mean more than a thousand words. For him, the emotional and mental symptoms will be as important as the general physical symptoms, if not more. This is quite the contrary in Western medicine, where the emotional aspect of the patient is left to be treated by psychiatrists and psychotherapists only.

### 6. The rules of homeopathic prescribing

Much of this is less interesting to the lay reader. However, Chapter Nine will discuss different potencies of remedies and how your homeopathic physician applies your remedies in which circumstances.

### 7. The theory of the miasms

This seventh rule was discussed in Chapter Five.


As you can see after reading about these pillars, homeopathy is not a matter of simply prescribing an antibiotic for colds. It does not try to get all the information about a patient through tons of lab tests and other diagnostics. The homeopath does not put a label on you: migraine, neuritis, arthritis, bursitis, etc.

But the homeopath does take notice of individual subtleties, of those special reactions particular to the patient himself. He does view every new patient as a unique being, completely different from anyone else. And these two people, patient and physician, become partners in the curative process. How challenging, how exciting! That is homeopathy.

May I give you a short quotation of the British Medical Association, years ago, on the training of its doctors in medical schools:

*"With our wider knowledge of scientific medicine we have tended to lose sight of general principles in a wealth of detail; the individual patient is limited to an interest in the disease with which we label him. One of the biggest defects in present day medical training is the failure to regard the patient as a whole. The student cannot be properly trained in this conception by the present method of dividing medicine into a number of distinct compartments taught separately."*

These very wise words unfortunately did not bring a change right away in the curriculum of their medical schools. But at least, one of Hahnemann's seeds is planted.

# CHAPTER NINE

# REMEDIES, DOSAGES AND OBSERVATIONS

*"No one can be a successful disciple of Hahnemann, who is not well versed, as Hahnemann himself was, in the learning of the medical schools; and it would be just as impossible for him to act judiciously without a knowledge of anatomy, physiology, pathology, surgery, together with chemistry and botany, as for a man, ignorant of navigation and seamanship, to carry a vessel with safety into port."*

*-- Constantin Hering, M.D.*

As I explained in the last chapter, there are many differences among practicing homeopaths. These differences are related mostly to which proponent of homeopathy they follow, or even which <u>version</u> of the master's theories they believe to be true. Those who adhere to Hahnemann's writings in the 6th edition of the *Organon* emphasize infinitesimal potencies of remedy ingredients, while those who extol Kent go with much higher potencies. In this chapter, I'll discuss these differences further and help you to understand the thinking behind remedy doses, and the observations and aggravations likely to appear with various remedies.

## How Much Is Too Much? The Question of Potency

Among themselves, homeopaths never seem to agree on what potency to use. There is a big group of Kentians, followers of James Kent, M.D., a Chicago-born physician in the mid - 19th century.  They are proponents of the high potency theory (because Kent followed Hahnemann's 5th edition of the <u>*Organon*</u>); most homeopaths fall into this category.  There are the Eizayaga followers, who recommend low potencies.  Eizayaga is an Argentine-born physician who uses prescriptions of 6C, 30C and 200C, which will be explained shortly. And finally there is a small, but growing group of LM prescribers. What does all this mean? If you have resolved to consult a homeopathic physician, what should you know about how to choose one appropriate for you? Are there advantages in one method over the other?

Dr. Kent had and still has an enormous influence on homeopathic prescribing. He adhered to Hahnemann's 5th edition of the <u>*Organon*</u>. So most "classical" homeopaths with their high-potency prescribing are practicing according to the 5th edition, not the 6th. However, in his last edition (the 6th), Hahnemann rejected "everything" he had written in the 5th edition and told his followers he had now "found his most perfect method," or the LM method.  Since homeopathy went into decline around 1925, the LM method was not sufficiently explored. Only now are practicing homeopaths marveling at the ingenuity of their master, Samuel Hahnemann.

Some homeopaths claim that Hahnemann never knew the advantages of high-potency prescribing, but this is not true. Hahnemann experimented with potencies at least as high as 1500C and according to Melanie, his wife, he knew and handled even higher potencies. Thousands of people of all classes flocked to Hahnemann in Paris; doctors practicing with him until the end of his life marveled at the ease with which he resolved complicated cases. But let me explain the differences in dosages and you can judge for yourself. Before I do this, what do 1x, 1C, 1M, and LM1 mean?

The homeopathic remedy containing the most molecules of the crude substance (usually an extract from a plant or mineral) is the tincture, also referred to as "mother tincture," or M.T.  The different botanical substances are soluble in alcohol of various strengths: 90%, 65%, 55% or 45%.  Tinctures should be used sparingly by the public: because of their potency, aggravations are often present.  Exceptions are the organ remedies, like Carduus for the liver, Apocynum and Crataegus (English

Hawthorne) for the heart, and Equisetum or horsetail for the kidney. It is less advisable to use products like Hydrastis or Golden Seal in tinctures. This marvelous remedy, repeated this way in a daily dose, would lead to unnecessary aggravations.

1x refers to one part or 0.10 gram of the crude substance dissolved in 1ml (one milliliter) of solution. So we have one part of substance versus ten parts of alcohol or Lactose, or 1/10.

1C refers to 0.01 gram of the crude substance or 1/100. So 1C is equal to 2x. If you know and understand these equivalencies, it will be easy for you to determine what potency you have to buy. If your doctor told you to get 6C and you see only 12x, you will know this is exactly the same. (Example: if 1C = 2x, then multiplying by 6, 6C = 12x.) 1M is equal to 1,000C, 10M to 10,000C, CM to 100,000C, MM to 1,000,000C. These are the high potencies used by Kentians.

LM1 is equal to 1/50,000C. As you can see, it goes completely the opposite way. (See Figure 1)

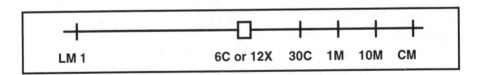

**Figure 1   Homeopathic Potencies**

## Kentian or High-Potency Prescribing

For a Kentian prescriber, 200C will be as low as he would go. But in the treatment of chronic diseases, he will be more inclined to start with 1M, which is equal to 1,000C. Contrary to what some homeopaths belief, 1M is the easiest, safest and gentlest of all high potencies. The 200C potency, on the other hand, is the most difficult to use. If the remedy was well chosen, a very good result follows. If wrong, a bad aggravation will assuredly occur.

## Advantages of High-Potency Prescribing

Because so many practitioners do advocate high-potency prescribing, there must be some reason for this. What is the advantage of this high potency prescribing? It has a deep, long-lasting action. The patient takes one dose and he does not have to repeat it for at least one month, or more, until his symptoms reoccur and his body tells him to repeat the dose. Compliance is assured. The physician does not have to interfere for the next month and telephone calls will be few since the physician and patient take the "wait and see" approach. However, disadvantages of this method can be enormous, as you will see below.

## Disadvantages of High-Potency Prescribing

One of the worst consequences is the almost ever-present aggravation. A <u>similar aggravation</u> is an aggravation of your already <u>existing</u> symptoms: it means you have the correct remedy but you need to adjust the dosage. With a high potency, the aggravation will be severe, and even more so if you are a sensitive person. A Kentian homeopath views this similar aggravation as a sign of success and encourages his patient to "weather the storm" since there is nothing he can do to alleviate the discomfort of his patient. He cannot adjust the dosage since it is already high and cannot be immediately repeated. This approach often translates as lack of empathy on the part of the physician and is diametrically opposed to what Hahnemann preaches in his 6th Edition of the <u>Organon</u>: the safe, rapid and gentle cure.

There is nothing gentle in going through days, sometimes weeks, of aggravation: many patients are lost in this critical time period, never to return to homeopathy. To those high prescribers, I would like to say: "Did you do what Hahnemann did, and deliberately test the remedies in high potencies on yourself? If not, you are no better than many allopathic doctors." Don't forget that although Hahnemann had about 10% of "sensitives" (patients reacting to environmental factors, see

Chapter Ten) under his care, it did not deter him from looking at improved, gentler methods.

Another danger in high-potency prescribing is the canceling out of the remedy while it is supposed to be working. For instance, you take your 1M today, and then drink your regular coffee, which may very well cancel the effect of the remedy. Both you and the physician would be waiting in vain for an improvement. At this point, management of the patient can become very difficult. The homeopathic physician has to impose strict guidelines on the patient: no peppermint or other mints, no coffee, camphor, lip balms, cough lozenges, tiger balm, nail polish or remover, electric blankets, recreational drugs or alcohol. While the latter should be avoided by any sensible person anyway, this instruction becomes more difficult with other products, especially prescription drugs.

A Kentian physician often says to a prospective client, "I can't treat you unless you are off all medications." This is very difficult for chronically ill patients who are on steroids, heart or hypertensive medication, etc. Some homeopaths go even further and forbid their clients to undergo other medical modalities such as massage, acupuncture, or supplement therapy. If anything, shiatsu, deep muscle massage, yoga, Qiqong, acupuncture and other hygienic measures do nothing but reinforce the alignment and balance of the patient, increasing his vital energy. With these types of regimens, the homeopathic remedy should work more, not less. By adhering to their prescribing, Kentian prescribers refuse many potential patients who could have been helped. To my mind, this is ignorant and does a disservice to patients and homeopathy alike!

**The LM Prescribers**

While Kentian homeopaths may call themselves "classical" homeopaths, the LM adherents are the only true "classical" practicing homeopaths. That's because they follow the guidelines established during the last ten years of Hahnemann's life. Let's not forget why the master of homeopathy did this. He was concerned with the severe reactions of some of his patients towards the homeopathic remedies. Realizing that long-lasting, severe aggravations would require a great effort from the patient's vital energy to overcome this, he kept on diluting his remedies. Not only did he greatly diminish aggravations, especially for hypersensitives, but he discovered that the diluted remedies worked better.

These lower potencies are a _must_ for sensitive people and no matter what medications the patient is on, he can start homeopathic treatment with LM potencies right away. Then, as the patient improves, you can diminish the amount of medication. There is no danger of the remedy being cancelled out, since the remedy is repeated in this dose _daily._ If by accident one dose was canceled, the remedy will be put in the patient's body again the next day. And there are many ways of adjusting the dose if the patient has an aggravation. By immediately adjusting dosages, such aggravations are minimal and short lasting, quite a difference with the high potencies. While these potencies are the best when you consult a homeopathic physician, what do you do at home for you more acute cases?

## Using Dosages at Home

It is useful to have a homeopathic physician as your instructor. However, this book can help you understanding the principles of homeopathy, and with the wide margin of safety of the remedies, this chapter and Chapter Eleven will teach you the wonderful first aid of homeopathy

The marvels of homeopathy are best demonstrated in the acute, everyday incidences: flus, colds, traumas, diarrhea, etc. But you may experience problems at home that either don't require that you visit your practitioner, or which happen on weekends or holidays. What should you have at home? A home remedy kit is described in Chapter Eleven. Here I want to discuss the potencies and how you should administer the remedy. For acute incidences you should have only 30C potencies. Chronic problems require the above mentioned LM or 6C potencies (which aren't as strong, but rely on steady dosages to accomplish their effects). But for everyday use, 30C's are a must.

How will you use them? I am going to give away the best kept secret in homeopathy: the water potencies. Usually, the doctor or homeopathic pharmacist will tell you to take three dry pellets twice a day, on or under the tongue. (By the way, there is no secret door under the tongue. This is a ritual stressed by some homeopaths.) A much better and cheaper way is to put **one** pellet of your remedy in 4 oz. of distilled water, let it dissolve, stir well and take a sip from this cup, every hour or as needed. This one cup with one pellet will be usable for 24 hours. After this, if you still need more of the remedy, make a new cup with one new pellet. For instance, if your child has sudden fever at midnight, Aconite (See Domestic Physician, Chapter Eleven) is indicated. Put one pellet Aconite in 4 oz. of water and give the child one sip. Check on the child 1/2 hour later. If he still has high fever or discomfort, give him another sip, and so on. You will see the miracle of homeopathy.

Why does the remedy work so much faster in water? Homeopathic remedies act through the nerves of the tongue. Homeopathy is a stimulative treatment: as soon as the little homeopathic pill touches the tongue, it sends a gentle shock throughout the nervous system, adding new energy to the reaction already started by your immune system or vital energy, against the invading enemy. It is not the same as taking medications sublingually where the first uptake is through the blood vessels. Homeopathic remedies work even when patients smell them or rub them on their skin. By dissolving the remedy in water, you spread its healing capacities over a bigger surface (water) which in turn can stimulate the tongue innervation more effectively.

## What Are Homeopathic Aggravations?

Almost any patient who has taken some remedy has either heard of or experienced the homeopathic aggravation. Aggravations occur in other forms of treatment as well. In Western medicine, we have the Herxheimer reaction (reaction of the body on intake of medications with fever, chills and discomfort, of short duration) and the side-effects of all the drugs. But homeopathic aggravations take two forms: the similar and the dissimilar.

### Similar Aggravations

A similar aggravation means that you feel an exacerbation of your existing symptoms. It indicates that you are using the right remedy, capable of curing your sick layer. The true homeopathic aggravation is when the patient says, "My symptoms are worse, but I feel better." But if this is the reaction you are having, it also means that your physician or you, the well-instructed patient, should adjust your dose immediately. If you are taking low potency remedies (6C or LM), you will stop taking your remedy for one or two days in which you will see that your symptoms disappear. Your body is simply using up the surplus remedy during the day(s) that you are not repeating it. You will feel better in the next days; only when you slightly aggravate, will you repeat the dose. As you can see, aggravations occur in matters of degree as well. A slight aggravation in this case is an indication to repeat the dose, whereas the first aggravation was an indication to back off from the dose. (See Figure 2). The second aggravation, which is less intense than the first, simply means that you have used up your remedy dose and repetition is necessary.

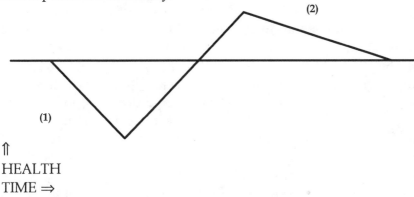

⇑
HEALTH
TIME ⇒

(1) = Aggravation because of too much medication
(2) = Aggravation because medication effect is depleted

**Figure 2**

### Dissimilar Aggravations

A dissimilar aggravation is bad news. After taking a homeopathic remedy, you immediately experience _new_, previously non-existent symptoms. This indicates that the wrong remedy has been recommended, and you should immediately stop the intake of your remedy and consult your physician.

When do aggravations appear? Much depends on the potency of the remedy. Low potency remedies might only show this aggravation after 14 days, after which you will adjust the dose . With Kentian potencies, there can be immediate and long lasting aggravation. Unfortunately you cannot adjust your dose (because it's given only once a month) and you have to weather the storm in the meantime. An antidote is not necessary because the similar homeopathic aggravation indicates a well chosen remedy.

### Ten Possible Aggravation Scenarios

What are other possible scenarios after taking a homeopathic remedy? (see Figure 3 on page 127)

**1. Immediate Improvement**: This is the first and best observation -- you see an immediate improvement in one or more of the signs of health (See Chapter One). If you notice an improvement of 50% after one week, slow down (just the opposite of what Western medicine would do). It's possible that you are going too fast with your car (your body and its healing) and that you will crash (experience an aggravation) soon. Start taking your remedy every two or three days instead of daily. Take the remedy as infrequently as you can while still holding a gradual level of improvement in your health. This will minimize the possibility of aggravation.

**2. No Reaction**: This is a situation in which there is no aggravation or improvement, even after two to three weeks. This can indicate either that the remedy is wrong or that there is something in your lifestyle that cancels the effects of the remedy (a road block on the path to recovery). The situation calls for review with your doctor. The roadblock should be removed <u>first</u> before any change in homeopathic remedy is made.

**3. Initial Improvement, then None**: The third scenario is that after initial improvement, no further improvement is made. You reach a plateau. Your doctor will have to discover the reason: either you need to increase the potency of the same remedy, or there is a miasm and an anti-miasmic remedy is needed, or the remedy has done all it could and a new remedy is needed. Consultation with your doctor is a must.

**4. Prolonged Aggravation and Decline**: In this fourth scenario, the patient experiences a prolonged aggravation and final decline. This means that there was no way to revive the vital energy of the patient. His was simply an incurable case.

**5. Quick Aggravation Followed by Improvement**: In this scenario, the patient's aggravation is quick and short, and is then followed by rapid improvement. This indicates an excellent prognosis and that the improvement will be long lasting.

**6. Immediate Improvement, Short-Lasting**: In this scenario, the patient immediately improves, but after a couple of days, each time the remedy is given, improvement is shortlasting. This indicates that the physician has not found the "true similimum," or that the remedy chosen was not close enough to the disease state. A better match must be sought. However, if it was a well-chosen remedy for the treatment of a chronic condition, this short amelioration of symptoms means that there is a structural change in the organs. The organs are damaged beyond repair and the homeopathic doctor can only assist in making the patient feel more comfortable.

**7. Reactions to Every Remedy**: This seventh scenario illustrates the case with hypersensitives (who are described in greater detail in Chapter Ten). As mentioned before, high potencies need to be avoided at any cost. LM potencies will be the best suited to people who react to every remedy they take.

**8. Symptom Improvement, But No Relief**: In this eighth scenario, it's most likely that the physician is only palliating the patient because, due to certain latent conditions, a longlasting deep cure is not possible. This will always be the case in scarring and partial destruction of the organs. The remedies act favorably, but there is only so much they can do.

**9. Longtime Improvement, Then Sudden Aggravation:** In this ninth scenario, the patient starts proving the remedy (in other words shows symptoms of his remedy which are similar to his old disease picture). It means that the patient is almost cured or at least the layer that the remedy was used for is almost dissolved. Stop the remedy at once, and wait. The aggravation will go away quickly and the patient will stay in an improved state for a long time. If there is another underlying layer, the patient's body will show the physician the next remedy that is needed. Old symptoms will reappear as new ones, and the physician selects a new, similar remedy. As mentioned in Hering's law, symptoms disappear in the reverse order of their appearance. In these instances, many times, <u>no</u> new remedy is needed. These old symptoms will disappear without any change of medicine. Unfortunately, many homeopaths don't recognize this and start prescribing new remedies and succeed only in fouling up the patient's progress.

**10. Disease Moves from Inside Out**: The tenth observation has to be with one of Hering's laws: diseases should go from the center of the body to its periphery. This is the hardest for the patient. He gets treated for arthritis, his pains disappear but then a skin rash appears. It is helpful to remember that this is a <u>favorable reaction,</u> and not to be tampered with. (See suppression, Chapter One). However, if you see superficial symptoms disappear and the patient showing organ symptoms, then the remedy is a wrong one. Change is needed immediately. The homeopathic physician, contrary to his modern, allopathic counterpart, will never select a remedy on external symptoms <u>alone</u>. This would only drive the disease inward and make the patient worse.

⇑ **signs of health**

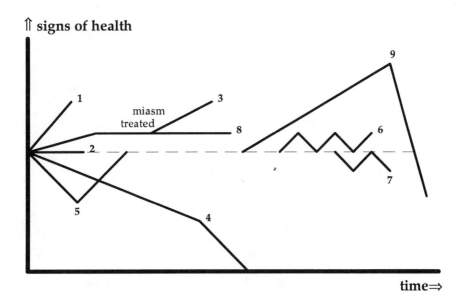

**time**⇒

Observations after the first dose intake of a homeopathic remedy

**Figure 3**

As you can see, treatment with homeopathic remedies is a lively, ever-changing picture. It requires from the patient that he get in tune with his body so as to recognize subtle changes, which are so important to communicate to his doctor. Once an effective homeopathic remedy is given, your body is in command and will tell you and your doctor <u>what to do next!</u>

# SECTION FOUR

## THERAPEUTIC INDICATIONS AND EXAMPLES:

## PUTTING HOMEOPATHIC THEORY TO PRACTICAL USE

# CHAPTER TEN

## SPECIAL TOPICS: ILLNESSES AND CONDITIONS OF OUR TIMES

In this and the next chapters, you'll be learning a lot about how to apply homeopathic thinking to your choice of remedies and doses. I can't stress enough how important it is that the physician help the patient make the choice of remedy; do not take it upon yourself to begin taking any remedy mentioned in this book without first consulting a responsible homeopathic physician. And again, should there be any doubt by what I mean by "responsible," I mean a homeopath practicing low-dose prescribing according to the 6th edition of Hahnemann's *Organon*.

### 1. The Hypersensitives

I have already mentioned in Chapter One the unfortunate example of the Universal Reactor (also called hypersensitives or people with environmental illness). Increasingly, the physician has to deal with patients whose sensitivity to environmental factors borders on the unbelievable. They're not only sensitive to cigarette smoke and perfumes but also react towards any fabric, chemical, environmental pollutants, animals, and even the recycled air in offices.

These patients become virtual prisoners of their environment. They are recluses in their own house where everything is stripped to the bare minimum: no carpets, no wallpaper, no sofas with leather or vinyl, no computers, printers, no gas stoves, no clothing with acrylic or other artificial fibers, no wall-to-wall carpeting, no TV, electric blankets, microwave oven, water bed, alarm clocks or radios. Nothing but hardwood floors, natural linoleum, natural cork, ceramic tile or marble; cotton or wool carpets which are void of toxic chemicals, 100% cotton clothes, which have to be washed with special detergents. Those patients cannot leave their houses without being overwhelmed by the toxicity of their environment.

The differentiation of mankind into "sensitives" and "non-sensitives" is of great practical import. The physician who does not recognize or accept this sensitivity will often play an inadequate role at the bedside of these patients. Modern medicine is slow to accept what Hahnemann recognized: it has labeled those patients as "hypochondriacs" and arrogantly denied the existence of such a problem. If those doubters could live for 24 hours in the skin of such a patient, they would understand the relentless suffering and isolation of people with Environmental Illness (E.I.). These victims have to fight ignorance and prejudice on top of an overwhelming affliction.

Sensitivity is an <u>exaggerated sensitiveness to stimuli</u>. The sensitive with his hyper-nervous perception has an openness to impressions not exhibited by the non-sensitive. According to their state of health or disease, they exhibit different reactions to external stimuli. What is hypo-stimulus (hypo = under or low) to one, becomes hyper-stimulus to the individual with great sensitivity. Stimuli that are normally perceptible and common to the healthy act upon the hyper-aesthetic person powerfully and abnormally. As Hahnemann showed in his 6th edition of the *Organon*, hypersensitives cannot be handled with high potencies. They will aggravate greatly. It was Hahnemann's compassion for the small number of hypersensitives in his time that led him to the LM potencies, the most perfect of them all. But even in our time, sensitives are daily becoming more common.

There are several methods by which sensitivity may be determined. It is not necessary to torture these patients with all kinds of allergy tests to establish a "scientific" basis for their diagnosis. A simple inquiry will suffice. Even the presence of the patient is not required, as knowledge gained from friends or family concerning the habits of the patient can be enough to establish the diagnosis. So who is sensitive and who is not?

### Symptoms of Sensitivity

In this section, I am not referring to the unfortunate E.I. patient, whose all-encompassing symptoms severely restrict his ability to relate to the world. Instead, I want to draw the attention to more subtle symptoms of sensitivity. We only have to point to the Signs of Health (Chapter One). Remember refreshed sleep? Non-sensitives, when well, sleep quietly all night, while sensitives are restless and given to insomnia. The more restless the sleep, the greater the sensitivity. They eat moderately and react to many environmental substances like perfumes and gasoline.

What is taken for granted by non-sensitives is a daily struggle for the sensitives. We can learn from their inclinations to seek a more simple life. The study of sensitives offers us concepts of primary importance.

Among the common signs of hyperaesthesia are anesthesia, numbness of fingers, arms, feet and legs. But the symptoms of the hypersensitive are best demonstrated by the two most common types: the **Arsenicum** type and the **Phosphorus** type. Incidentally, these are the two main remedies (besides Mercury Sol., see later in this chapter) in homeopathy for hypersensitives. As always, the remedy is selected according to the laws of homeopathy explained in Chapter Eight.

### The Arsenicum Hypersensitive

There is no bigger "hypochondriac" in homeopathy than the Arsenicum type. Don't misunderstand me. Hypochondria is not as demeaning a term to the homeopath as it is for the modern doctor. It merely reflects the great anxiety and fear these patients have for death, disease and contamination. Because of their condition, they see everything around them as an enemy, and they feel (rightfully so) that they cannot handle more stress on their precious vital energy, not even the slightest flu. They are very restless, emotionally and physically, but because of great fatigue, are unable to move around a lot. They are typically very chilly, looking for a warm source to be close to. They despair about their recovery, and their future in which they foresee nothing but poverty and isolation. They are very tidy but their great weakness does not always allow them to be obsessive about it. They are thirsty for cold water which they drink in little sips. They can be capricious and nasty.

What are some of the causes of hypersensitivity in this patient? A financial loss (for example, the stock market crash); food-poisoning and any other substance that was a poison to the body; exposure to chemicals, breast implants, poisoning by over-medication (i.e., an illness that is iatrogenically induced).

### The Phosphorus Type

While the Arsenicum type exhibits great sensitivity to foods, phosphorus types are more reactive to environmental factors: perfumes, gasoline, newsprint, "sick-buildings," (where the constantly recyled air, formaldehyde-treated carpets and building materials do damage to the immune system) and the electro magnetic fields (EMF) of electrical power lines, radio, TV, alarm clocks, water beds and electric blankets, microwave ovens, etc. This is the longilineal (tall and thin) type, hypersensitive to noise, light and smells. They are euphoric, creative dreamers and always have new interests. They are wonderful starters, but poor finishers because they run out of steam. They are individuals who can prophesize weather changes, becoming restless and fearful as storms approach. They are very sentimental, vain and talkative and are very psychic and clairvoyant. Possible causes of this type of sensitivity are too-rapid growth, a bout with hepatitis, loss of fluids, ill effects from grief and anger, physical and emotional over-exertion or an anesthesia or a pneumonia, after which they were never well since.

In general, one can determine sensitivity or non-sensitivity in a patient by looking at the way he conducts himself in life. Liveliness, fineness of feeling, restlessness, desire for change of work or interest, capriciousness, and a less well-balanced mental state are marks of the sensitive. It is also interesting to see how, in a dark room, sensitives never seem to stumble against a wall or furniture. It is important for the physician to remember that there are great differences in patients in the degree of sensitivity: some patients get teeth extracted without anesthesia, while others faint at the sight of the injection needle. The regular school of medical thought has bothered itself very little with these differences. It will be up to the homeopathic physician to study the problem of sensitivity more carefully, and determine the right potencies for our remedies. The LM potencies are the answer to the prayer of the sensitive patient, as their flexibility allows the physician to find the right dose no matter how sensitive the patient is.

## 2. Mercury Intoxication

In December 1990, 60 *Minutes*, CBS's nationally televised feature program, aired an excellent survey of the mercury dental filling controversy. The American Dental Association is adamant that mercury fillings are non-toxic and completely safe. However, many countries in Europe (Sweden, Germany) have banned the use of mercury after clinical reports indicated that mercury fillings are toxic and may lead to brain damage. The big question is: how can you know in advance whether removal of your mercury fillings will benefit you? Removal of mercury, depending on the amount you have in your mouth, can cost you thousands of dollars.

Homeopathy has the answer. The effects of mercury are well-known through the proving Hahnemann did with metallic mercury. In other words, mercury fillings are a problem if you have some of the following symptoms:

- Foul-smelling breath with metallic taste
- Presence of a geographic tongue (changes on the tongue that resemble a map)
- Imprints of teeth on the sides of the tongue
- Recurrent presence of canker sores or herpes sores within the mouth
- Bleeding, receding gums with tendency to ulceration

- Heavy salivation with intense thirst
- Abscessed teeth
- Trembling tongue: the tongue quivers, like a snake's tongue
- Recurrent pharyngitis (inflamed throat) with swollen glands

Notice that all the symptoms listed above are located in the mouth.  It is precisely there that we have the highest concentration of mercury in the dental fillings, causing many of the above mentioned symptoms.  But there are others:

- Severe weakness and fatigue
- Recurrent colds: because of lack of adequate defenses, these patients  catch everything
- Great sensitivity to warmth and cold: the patient is a human barometer and has a difficult time finding the right temperature
- Excessive sweating at night
- Brainfag and weak memory
- Chills and fevers
- Volatile nature -- mercurial, changeable, impulsive
- Worries and has great anxiety about health
- Highly sensitive to the environment (See above, Arsenicum type of hypersensitives)

Is extraction the only therapy possible?  In case you have doubts and hesitate to spend thousands of dollars to change all your mercury fillings, you could take Mercury Solubilis 6x, 3 pellets twice a day for at least one month and see if your symptoms improve.  If they improve, this means you do have mercury poisoning and would benefit from extraction.  If decide to have all your mercury fillings extracted, you will be surprised to see that you might have an aggravation of your symptoms at first.  The dentist will tell you that this is due to release of a certain amount of mercury into the bloodstream.  What he will not tell you is that you can prevent these uncomfortable reactions by taking Merc. Sol. 30C before and after the procedure.  Take three pellets before the removal and three pellets after the removal.   If the dentist decides to take the mercury out in different stages, repeat the procedure.

As usual, prevention is the best therapy.  In case you need a new filling,   ask your dentist to use inorganic cement or porcelain.  You will save yourself a lot of trouble!

## 3.  CFIDS: The Mysterious Disease

After reading the preceding chapters, you already understand that looking for a "mysterious virus" as the cause of CFIDS is a waste of time.  Researchers at three medical centers in New Jersey, Massachusetts and Colorado are currently conducting "sophisticated" tests on patients with Chronic Fatigue Syndroke.  But as I already mentioned above, these tests are only aimed at detecting measurable molecular and pathological changes, not at the whole person.  Why is it that the immune system cannot clear the many viruses in its body?  Why are cytokines abnormally activated in these patients?  (Cytokines are cells of the immune system that have been isolated and turned into drugs to fight cancer, so far without any earth-shaking results.)  All modern researchers do is look at the patient in every way they can, noting the consequences.  While the air continues to leak from the hole in the balloon (the patient), modern researchers focus on what the deflated balloon looks like, instead of trying to repair the hole.

We need to look at the patient when he was in his beginning stage of the disease, and try to get an idea about his simple change of state before his health was compromised.  How can we expect to treat the disease in an intelligent way if we do not know what the beginnings are?  I am not saying that the physician can know too much about the endings of disease, because post-mortem examinations do have their place in medicine.   But to think that the findings of an autopsy and examinations of organs as well as the results of lab tests will help the physician to prescribe for sick people is a great folly!

In Chapter Four, I outlined many emotional factors leading to a state of chronic exhaustion.  All of them are possible causative factors of CFIDS and need to be repaired with homeopathic remedies if we want to be successful in fighting this disease. Of course you have the other factors: the miasms (discussed in Chapter Five), and mercury intoxication (See above). But there are other triggers of "weakness." Don't forget, we view a diseased state as a <u>decrease in vital energy</u>. Once this energy has reached a certain low level, the patient is susceptible to viruses, bacteria, yeast and parasites, which are consequences, <u>not</u> causes. When are we going to learn in Western medicine to put the horse before the cart, not behind it? It is this attitude that makes us lose the battle against cancer, AIDS and other serious chronic disease.

One possible cause of CFIDS is what we in homeopathy call <u>ailments due to a loss of fluids</u>. This can be a loss of semen through excessive sexual activity, excessive masturbation or nightly, spontaneous emissions. The Chinese too recognized the weakening of the body through loss of what they called the "most precious or ancestral Qi" (the seminal fluid) and told stories about the Chinese Emperor who slept with young women without having an ejaculation, thus capturing their orgasm.

Besides the sexual fluids, excessive loss of other bodily fluids -- through chronic diarrhea, excessive menstrual bleeding, breastfeeding or excessive sweating -- can contribute to loss of energy. I remember a case I had in which the patient was dripping sweat from his hands and head for many years. This constituted a huge loss of energy. That was the sole reason for his chronic fatigue, which was easily repaired by homeopathy. The main remedies for loss of fluids in general are cinchona and Phosphoric Acid, although they are not the only ones.

Then there are ailments from <u>exposure to certain climate factors</u>. The main enemy of the immune suppressed patient is *dampness*. We already mentioned the sycosis miasm with its high sensitivity to humidity (Chapter Five). Any CFIDS patient will have aggravated symptoms when there is much humidity in the air or right after the rain stops falling. Of course, any other climate factor in excess, be it cold, dryness, wind or heat will do the same thing. A person who says he was "never well since a sunstroke," which often causes headaches, weakness and diarrhea, should respond to Glonoin or Veratrum Album.

There are many more causes of a decrease of vital energy. The main point that I want to make here is that there is no single virus nor any other single cause responsible for such a complex disease like CFIDS. Pursuing such a road of inquiry amounts to ignorance and a waste of time and money while creating false hope. Instead, look at Figure 4, which displays an overview of true etiologic factors of CFIDS, which is the umbrella name for Candida, EBV, CMV, HHV viruses, Herpes simplex viruses, etc.

Another source of confusion about CFIDS patients is their apparent immunity to flus and colds. How many times have I heard these patients say, " My immune system must not be too bad, I never get the flu like everyone around me." There is a perfect explanation for this in the Law of Dissimilars and Similars. This law states that *"Dissimilar diseases repel each other, while similar ones attract and cure each other."* What does this mean? Even during violent epidemics of flu and colds, the number of CFIDS victims who contract the disease is relatively small. The reason is that the CFIDS disease is so virulent and strong that a little flu virus cannot suppress a strong dissimilar disease like CFIDS. In most CFIDS victims a war is already raging between the immune system and many virulent viruses, bacteria and yeast cells. In other words, the strong CFIDS picture cannot be suppressed by the epidemic flu virus.

However, when the CFIDS case is mild or has been greatly healed, then the virulent flu microbe will be able to suppress the CFIDS symptoms temporarily! In other words, the patient feels the flu symptoms while most of his CFIDS symptoms are suppressed -- when the flu microbe is conquered, the CFIDS symptoms come back in the same intensity as before. This indicates that the CFIDS condition has never left the body. Two dissimilar diseases cannot cure each other. Hence, CFIDS patients who never got the flu before and all of a sudden do get it, should almost rejoice since it reflects a less severe stage of their CFIDS.

On the other hand, when two similar diseases meet together in the body, they can cure the existing picture. The law further states that *"two similar diseases cannot coexist in the body, only the stronger will survive and create the clinical picture."* For instance, if you had swollen glands and a sore throat for a long time, and you now are the victim of a flu whose characteristics are

FIGURE 4: TRUE ETIOLOGIC FACTORS OF CFIDS

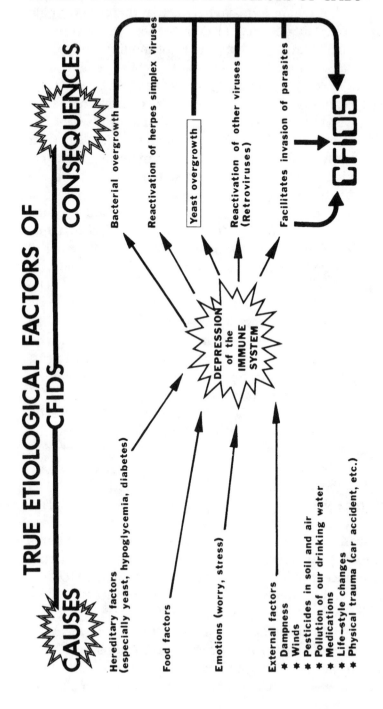

*On the left appear various co-factors, which, if present in sufficient numbers, will weaken the immune system, leaving it vulnerable to a variety of immune-suppressed conditions, and finally CFIDS.*

very similar in nature, your sore throat and swollen glands will disappear <u>permanently</u> while your symptoms will be those of the flu epidemic. This observation in nature should teach allopathics the best ways to cure: according to the laws of similars, not the opposites!

It is not my goal to repeat everything here about CFIDS that has been covered in my book, <u>Full of Life</u>. I refer you to that text if you think you may have this condition.

## 4. Marijuana Intake: Helpful or Harmful?

I am surprised to see that some patients, while struggling to regain their health, are oblivious to obvious toxic factors like drugs. But where cocaine, heroin, and LSD rightfully have a bad reputation, most people view the occasional use of marijuana as innocent, even necessary, for their lifestyle. But be aware, users. It is not the little innocent, make-me-feel-good drug you want to believe it is. It can be an obstruction to cure. In acupuncture, marijuana is believed to create "heat-dampness" in the body, hence disrupting the fine balance between the liver (your immune system) and spleen/pancreas (your digestive system). Again, homeopathy gives a more refined portrait of what really happens to you when you consume repeated doses of marijuana or cannabis sativa. This cannabis drug picture is being extensively and voluntarily proved by large segments of the population, especially teenagers and young adults, and others from the '60s generation. What are the symptoms or consequences of repeated use?

One peculiar symptom is the <u>slowing of passage of time</u>, so that minutes seem like hours. This is most likely related to the slowing of the pulse, although the opposite is also possible. Ingestion of marijuana can either raise or lower the blood pressure and produce chilliness or heat, especially in hands and feet.

Another area affected by cannabis is the genito-urinary tract, where irritation and inflammation in the bladder, prostate and urethra can be experienced. In addition, cannabis can either stimulate or depress sexual desire and fertility in either sex. Studies have even shown decreased motility of sperm and reduction of sperm count in males who use marijuana.

Cannabis can also induce paranoia and hallucinations, fear of loss of control, and out-of-body experiences that terrorize the patient, and "spaciness" in general. Ataxia in coordination, confusion, tremors, and dizziness are other symptoms of repeated intake of marijuana.

By the same token, cannabis sativa can be an excellent remedy <u>used in homeopathic doses</u>. In former times it was used as a treatment for gonorrhea and it can be used for urethritis, cystitis and prostatitis. And don't forget, the curative power of herbs, drugs, and vitamins implies the existence of hypersensitive individuals who become ill from minute doses. So these can be used in patients with the above mentioned symptoms who "never have been well since intake of marijuana."

# 5. Vaccinations and Epidemic Diseases

I am sure to stir up some controversy in this section. However, what I want to present is a critical look at the immunization controversy. <u>I do not want to recommend against or for vaccinations</u>. When it comes to your health and that of your children, you have to take personal responsibility, and the best way to do that is by gathering as much information as you can. After carefully reading this chapter, I trust that you will want to do some more research on your own. It's essential that you seek out the objective opinions from both sides. This will enable you to make the decision that is right for <u>you</u>. In this section of the chapter, I will be presenting some of my own beliefs about vaccinations and epidemic diseases.

### Compulsory Vaccinations: A Fact of Life?

There is something that started to bother me about vaccinations almost as soon as I started administering them to my patients. As a "holistic" doctor I had a hard time accepting the fact that people did not have free choice in making the decision about vaccinations. More and more of my patients, call them "New-Age" if you want, started to question the validity of systematic vaccination of their babies at the prime age of three months. Some refused to allow any vaccination for their child, only to go head to head later with school principals who are required by law to demand proof of vaccination as a condition of school enrollment. Most of the mothers did not have the necessary grit to defy existing school laws but that did not diminish the agony about the decision to vaccinate their children.

After all, look at what vaccinations really are: the injection of foreign substances or live viruses into the bloodstream of entire populations. From what we know about bacterial flora and the viral microcosmos, it is not their mere presence that produces a menace to mankind, but rather the <u>upsetting of their natural balance</u>. It scares me to think of what the consequences are of eradicating entire populations of microbial species, all in the name of medical progress. In fact, whenever a new disease comes up, often our first thought is of preparing a possible vaccination. Look at AIDS, different cancers, the yearly flu, etc. If we, as a population, are required to get inoculated, then we are at least entitled to <u>convincing proof</u>, beyond any reasonable doubt, that these immunizations are safe and effective.

### Are Vaccinations Effective?

For most people and physicians, this is a superfluous question. Haven't we seen a remarkable decline in the prevalence of once-feared epidemic diseases? Haven't some diseases such as smallpox entirely disappeared from the face of the earth? So then, what's the question about? Let's look at the real facts. Maybe we are worshipping our own ability to manipulate nature, without looking at the reality. Before we <u>assume</u> that the decline of certain epidemics is entirely related to the use of vaccines, we'd better look at the fact that some of these natural diseases were already on the decline, following their own natural course, <u>independent</u> of drugs and vaccines.

Diseases such as whooping cough, diphtheria, tetanus, cholera and polio had begun to decline long before any of those vaccinations were introduced. Most likely, improved hygienic measures had the biggest impact. Was humankind adapting to surrounding enemies without the help of antibiotics or vaccinations? We should recognize that mankind and the animal kingdom alike live peacefully with our most notorious microbial foes. It is commonly understood that infection can occur without producing disease, as we see over and over again in the typical childhood diseases, such as measles, polio, rubella, etc.

The next disturbing fact is that infections of all kinds keep on breaking out in populations that were <u>immunized against them!</u> Even more, the difference in incidence in the vaccinated and non-vaccinated population has been minimal, even negligible. In other words, in every part of the world where outbreaks of infectious diseases happened, even fully immunized children contracted the disease in fairly large numbers without lower rates in death and complications. How can we explain this? Using common sense, we could postulate that immunizations only give <u>partial or short-lasting immunity</u>. Since vaccinations are made from attenuated viruses, we could easily suspect that they elicit a short antibody response. This "wearing off" effect would then require boosters at regular intervals to maintain the immunity of the person. But how often do we need to give these boosters? How long is temporary immunity in each individual? There is no way to know, taking into account the intrinsic differences in characteristics and sensitivities of each person.

Do not think that vaccines produce only a weakened copy of the original disease. All vaccines commonly produce symptoms of their own. Physicians routinely warn their patients to look for common side-effects like fevers, irritability in the child, loose stools, etc. For instance, the pertussis vaccine is probably one of the major causes of "fever of unknown origin" in small children today. This is a sign of disturbance of the vital energy in the patient, not acknowledged by most doctors. But it sure gets the attention of everyone involved when the child comes down with encephalitis, leukemia, cortical blindness and many other severe conditions.

In homeopathy we have a rubric, "<u>never well since vaccinations,</u>" which contains the different remedies against ill effects of vaccines. Often these ill consequences are hard to recognize. I remember such a case in my practice. This patient had been a healthy, upbeat, sportive yoga teacher, who had become tired, allergic to many substances, and was having memory disturbances. In short, she exhibited many of the symptoms of what we see in a Chronic Fatigue Syndrome patient, which was her "diagnosis." Unfortunately this was before the time I studied homeopathy and I could not help her. As it happened, she had received the mandated flu shot before becoming a teacher in college, and she had never been the same since. She became very despondent and eventually committed suicide. It is something that I will always regret -- not having learned quickly enough about homeopathy.

At the same time, it horrifies me to think about the thousands of flu shots given to the population, especially to children and elderly with existing risks, the so-called "high risk groups." I wonder how many become victims of these shots?

### Vaccinations and Immune Malfunctions

It is obvious that vaccines have not always given us protection against acute illnesses. Let's look at what happens in common childhood diseases such as measles, chickenpox, and rubella. When one of these viruses is inhaled (most of the time, the respiratory tract is the port of entry into the body), there is a latency period during which the patient shows no symptoms. This period lasts often from 7 to 14 days, and during this time-span the virus multiplies in the tonsils, adenoids, and lymph nodes <u>before</u> it passes into the bloodstream. It is carried throughout the lymph system. By the time the patient shows the first symptoms, circulating antibodies against the virus are formed, the result of the mounting effort by the ingenious immune system. The result is that the child will never have the same childhood disease again and is then prepared to respond more promptly to any other infection.

In contrast, when we use vaccines and inject them directly into the bloodstream, bypassing the normal port of entry (the respiratory tract), the weakened virus will not cause the long incubation period at the tonsils and adenoids and will not initiate any generalized inflammatory response, so important in helping us to fight infection in general.

What happens to those injected virus particles of the vaccine? Do they persist for prolonged periods of time, or even permanently in the system, leading to *suppression* of the immune system? We just don't know the answers to these questions yet. But artificial immunization only focuses on a single aspect of the immune process: antibody formation. It is obvious that if we fail to imitate nature well with our vaccines, they will fall short of our expectations.

This brings up another question. Why are we seeing such a dramatic increase in autoimmune disorders in which the patient forms antibodies against his own tissues? Diseases such as lupus, multiple sclerosis, Hashimoto's disease (a thyroid condition), Crohn's disease, ulcerative colitis, and rheumatoid arthritis are diagnosed in increasing, frightening numbers. Why? Could it be that the existence of these foreign proteins of the vaccines play a role? It is easy to see that if these proteins exist for a long time in the human body, that the immune system must try to continue to make antibodies against it, leading to a hyper-stimulation of the defense system.

Since the virus is incorporated within the genetic material of our cells, antibody formation will be directed against our own cells. These mysterious autoimmune disorders make a lot more sense if we recognize that in order to preserve "health," destroying the chronically infected cells is the only way to clear these foreign antigenic materials before they become a threat to life in general. And yet, for any new disease that crops up, be it AIDS or cancer, the quest for a new vaccine is on. The latest medical news is about the attempt to manufacture an immune response in cancer patients by injecting cultivated numbers of the patient's own white blood cells in lab dishes and give them back to the patient as medicine. Here we see the first law of homeopathy, "Like cures like" (see Chapter Eight). The problem will be determining the right amount of tumor antigens. Perhaps the homeopathic practice of using <u>minute doses</u> would be effective here?

### Homeopathy and Epidemics

We all know that vaccines are supposed to cut down the incidence of epidemics of infectious diseases. The yearly flu vaccination, thrust on the ignorant public, is a perfect example. Every year, a flu vaccination is prepared from known existing viruses with the hope that they will be active against future new epidemics. Knowing the dangers of vaccines in general, what would be a better approach?

The homeopath following the laws and principles of his method, has no difficulties in dealing with any new upcoming epidemic. This was proven over and over again during the last 200 years. During the great flu epidemic of 1918, the death rate in English hospitals of people treated with homeopathic remedies was a mere 2% versus 50% treated with regular medicines. How does the homeopath treat people when a new epidemic breaks out? If an epidemic is entirely different from anything that has yet appeared (and this happens almost every year), the situation at first can appear confusing. But as more victims of the flu are seen, the homeopathic physician writes down all the different symptoms he has seen in his flu victims, and thus will be able to identify the essential features of this epidemic. With the aid of his repertory, the homeopathic physician will be able to find the five or so remedies related to the epidemic and which cover all of its symptoms. In this way, Hahnemann was able to administer the homeopathic remedy for more severe epidemics (i.e. typhoid fever, scarlatina) to the rest of the family as a preventative.

In the winter of 1992-1993, we experienced in the United States a flu characterized by a severe sore throat, followed by bronchial involvement -- patients were coughing up copious amounts of yellow-green mucus. Regardless of whether it was treated by antibiotics or not, the condition lasted for three weeks. After seeing about 20 patients with similar symptoms, I could clearly distinguish two remedies covering this flu epidemic: Gelsemium and Mercury Solubilis. It made my diagnosis of the next cases very easy and administering one of these two remedies aborted the flu within a couple of days. What a saving of vital energy for the patient! And all this at a very cheap price and with no endangerment of the patient's life.

This also applies to new epidemics of "old forgotten" diseases that are cropping up in alarming numbers and which do not respond to our existing antibiotics. In 1992, more than 26,000 new cases of tuberculosis were reported nationwide, most of them resistant to existing treatment. There is a growing number of patients infected with strains of TB that are resistant to standard drugs. Again, by aiming only at the microorganism involved, Western medicine fails to prevent the comeback of many deadly diseases. Homeopathy, because it focuses on the totality of symptoms rather than the pathology, does not face that problem. The homeopath will look at the case, carefully noting down the general, mental and peculiar characteristics of the case and have at his disposal several healing remedies. Thousands of new cases of resistant gonorrhea and syphilis are making their way back into the population. Together with the new epidemics like AIDS, it will force modern medicine to look at alternative medicines.

Coming back to the subject of our mandatory vaccines, how do we recover from the ill-effects of vaccines? The "never well since a vaccination" rubric contains several marvelous remedies: Silica, Thuja, Ledum, Malandrinum, Medorrhinum, Pyrogen, Apis, Arsenicum, Psorinum and Sulphur are just a few. One of these will be prescribed according to the kind of vaccination and the clinical picture that is presented.

Another weapon against infectious diseases is the <u>nosode</u>. Nosodes are different diseased animal products used as remedies. We have Variolinum (for smallpox), Morbillinum (for measles), Tuberculinum (TB), Syphilinum (Syphilis) just to name a few. Many homeopaths use them en lieu of vaccinations. We can make nosodes for most of the vaccines, pertussis included.

The idea that we could find solutions for all human suffering is attractive, but is a myth -- as human beings we are at risk for disease and death at every moment. The vaccination is merely an experiment that may have caused endless amounts of sickness and suffering. To prove that this is so should not be required of those who oppose their use. Rather, to prove that it is <u>not</u> so should certainly be demanded of those who would and do advocate vaccinations. Anything less is a crime, reminding us of many medical tragedies we have seen in the past, where advocates of a procedure exaggerate its positive values and conceal the dangers. Remember the tragedies with medications like thalidomide (prescribed as an anti-nausea medication for pregnant mothers and which caused horrible birth defects) or the breast implants, practiced without safety tests on thousands of people? Can we afford another tragedy, practiced on almost the entire population?

## 6. Addictions: How Homeopathy Helps

### 1. Alcoholism

Alcoholism is a curse that has been with mankind since the dawn of civilization. Be it family breakup, economic problems, hereditary predisposition or simply boredom, alcoholism has not let up in our time. Hundreds of thousands of people suffer from it, and countless more are its direct and indirect (family) victims. Western medicine, in spite of large TV and radio public relations campaigns, has had no permanent success dealing with alcoholism. The familiar pattern of remission and relapse seen in patients treated in detoxification centers is largely a result of the changeable resolve of the patient to follow through on his plan. Another reason for failure is that most of these plans look at the endings, not the beginnings. Emotional and family conflicts are certainly some of the underlying problems which must be probed and repaired, something for which Western medicine is not very well equipped.

The alcoholic is "addiction prone." The best proof is seen in the large support group meetings of Alcoholics Anonymous (AA), where people have switched from alcohol to coffee and cookies. But this is still better than trying to control the alcohol addiction with medications. The use of medications weakens our desire to achieve self-confidence and inner balance, a key to resolving any addiction. Support and help from other individuals in AA meetings is essential, while an adequate vitamin supported diet is a must if a cure is to be achieved. Vitamin B-12 injections, liver injections, Vitamin C, B-6 and niacin are helpful aids. But all these measures seldom work alone.

Besides a support network and vitamin therapy, a third pillar of support that is needed is a well-chosen homeopathic remedy. There are two important points to be considered. First, in the choice of remedy, the homeopathic physician should note the intellectual and moral symptoms presented by the patient. For this purpose, it will be essential to talk to the immediate family who can give a description of the behavior of the patient under the influence of alcohol. Prescribing a remedy by consulting the person only when sober will mislead the physician.

I have seen several types of alcoholics. One of the major groups of alcoholics is the secretive drinker. I remember such a case in my clinic. The onset of his problem was job stress-related. His wife told me that he became indifferent to her, and did not want to bathe or otherwise attend to his personal hygiene. He worked long hours, feeding himself alcohol and junk food, and his skin looked dirty and unhealthy. His alcoholism affected all parts of his social and emotional life. Sulphur is an excellent remedy for secretive drinkers, and worked very well for the person described.

Another patient of mine started drinking after the death of his wife. They had been married for 30 years and were very close to each other. He drank only by himself in the evening, and when drunk, he cried easily. He did not want company, never went to bars and felt very unhappy with himself. This is the drinker who is lonely and cold, who finds solace in alcohol. The alcohol kills the pain, and "gives him courage" to face the next day. Conium is often very helpful in this situation.

Other people are more the "angry" types of alcoholics. They drink until late at night, come home late and wake up in the morning with a terrible hang-over. They are in a foul mood and family members understand that this person cannot be spoken to until the afternoon hours. They are constipated, love rich and fatty foods and need coffee as a stimulant if alcohol is not available. This is a typical Nux Vomica picture, often helpful in D.T.'s or Delirium Tremens attacks.

Many more remedies can be indicated: homeopathic opium for people who go to sleep while drinking; Staphysagria for people addicted to sex, masturbating during drinking episodes; Arsenicum for the cramps and diarrhea seen in acute attacks; Chelidonium, phosphorus, Lycopodium, Sulphuric acid and China for liver disorders resulting from drinking. But besides the indicated remedy, a must for every alcoholic is Avena Sativa or the common oat plant, administered in tincture: 5 drops two to three times a day (Note: tinctures are given in a dosage of 5 drops three times a day in water). Another homeopathic remedy to reduce or eliminate the alcohol cravings is Ledum. It is indicated in alcoholics with red face, red pimples on the forehead, a red blotchy nose and bloated skin. Use it in 30C potency, twice a day.

Often, the alcoholic who takes pleasure in his vices and does not want to be cured can be helped anyway. Family members can slip the indicated homeopathic remedy in his drink, as this produces in the patient a natural tendency to healing with a sense of reason, duty and the willpower to achieve success. The remedies, of course, cost practically nothing compared with social programs and detoxification centers.

The economic value of homeopathy becomes even more important in this day and age, where politicians are looking for solutions to cut the ever-growing costs of health care. Not all patients following this program will have success, as nothing is absolute. But the patient's chances are increased enormously by working together with a competent homeopath. Can you imagine what an influence a successful homeopathic treatment would have on alcohol-related crimes such as those related to drunk driving, robbery committed to support drinking habits, and crimes of passion committed under the influence of alcohol?

### 2. Other "drug addictions"

I already have outlined the dangers of the "innocent" ingestion of marijuana. Much of what has been said for alcoholism is relevant for other drug addictions. Avena Sativa is a must for other drug addictions. As usual, the physician has to make a detailed interview that includes non-judgmental acceptance, directness and persistence, something a homeopathic physician is well trained in. Other herbs useful with drug addicts are Valerian tincture, especially in the victim who shows symptoms of sleeplessness with jerking of the limbs, hallucinations at night, cramps and diarrhea (5 drops three times a day of this tincture in water will help). _Passiflora_ is another calming herb used in the same way.

Serious consideration must be given to why the patient started on the road to addiction. Was it abandonment, a broken heart, low self confidence, a severe grief, fears, loneliness or a disappointment in a career? Each of these causes can be covered by an appropriate homeopathic remedy and, administered with care, should help the patient on the way to recovery.

And then, we have the big group of coffee addicts. "It's the only thing that gets me out of bed and to the office!" "I can give up anything but please don't take my coffee away." Sound familiar? You are not alone. Coffee is so well-accepted that most people don't think about coffee as an addiction.

Remember the signs of health in Chapter One? You are supposed to wake up _refreshed_. Failure to do so should encourage you to look for the _real_ cause of your fatigue, not for the pot of coffee to "jump start your engine." But there is help for anyone who wants to make a serious attempt. Angostura in homeopathic dosage helps quiet the overwhelming cravings for coffee. But what about those awful coffee withdrawal reactions (or any other drug withdrawal reaction)? The best remedy to help you with your irritability and moodiness during this withdrawal is Chamomilla 30C: take 3 pellets twice a day. Other helpful remedies, in descending order of effectiveness, are Nux Vomica 30C and Coffea 30C or potentized coffee. Together with Avena Sativa tinctures, anyone who wants to go off his "drugs" will be greatly helped. You will be surprised how much easier it will be to keep your New Year's resolution to finally quit the caffeine habit.

Addictions to sugar and chocolate are approached in the only possible way and that is looking at the person as a whole. Is there bloating, gas, constipation, craving for fresh air, abdominal distention, hypoglycemia with those incredible sweet cravings? Argentum nitricum or Lycopodium can be indicated.

Undeniably, homeopathy should be used in every detox center and in every household where an addictive person lives. It is cheap, easy to administer and more effective than the western drugs available. The last thing a physician should do to an addict is replace one drug addiction with another.

## 7. Geriatric Problems

Homeopathy has much to offer geriatric patients. The gentleness, lack of side effects and the fast action of homeopathic remedies is especially appreciated in the individual whose vital energy is minimal or has been damaged during the course of his or her life. The last thing these patients need are mood-altering, suppressive medications, robbing them and their families alike of their last joyful years together. The following sections recommend the best homeopathic approaches to some common problems of aging. Again, consultation with your physician regarding treatment for these conditions is a <u>must.</u>

### 1. Prostate cancer: stealth cancer

Prostate cancer strikes without warning and affects 1 out of 10 men in the United States. Increased life expectancy for the general population has brought increased prevalence of this dreaded killer. Doctors advise every man above 50 to have an annual prostate exam but the reality is that not even 10% will do so, mostly because of the discomfort associated with the digital rectal exam. While this simple exam tops the list of the recommended screenings, a new blood test, the <u>PSA</u>, or Prostatic Specific Antigen, has given some new hope and has boosted the chances of early detection. Like anything else, it is not foolproof. It misses at least 20% of the tumors and often gives a false positive test. Sometimes the PSA test is positive while the clinical exam is negative. There have been cries for mass screening with this PSA test but in my opinion they are unfounded. Many prostate tumors are benign and slow-growing and much unnecessary treatment would take place.

What does modern medicine offer? For years, surgery was the advocated therapy but had one unwanted side effect: impotence. Fortunately, an improved technique which spares the nerves has eliminated this problem for the most part. Radiation (about 35 sessions) is another heralded therapy. Female hormone therapy has been given to people with cancer spread to the bone; however, besides the many side effects (decreased libido, breast growth) it does not really cure the cancer.   As usual, allopathic medicine has many ways to treat the disease with strong suppressive therapies, but not many strategies to avoid it. Often, urologists simply tell their patients to "live with their benign prostate adenoma till the symptoms get bad enough that they want to do something about it."

However, there are other treatments besides antibiotics for prostatitis (inflammation of the prostate) sufferers.   Sabal serrulata 3x or Salm Palmetto, a plant, is often called the "homeopathic catheter" because it relieves congestion.   It is recommended for anyone suffering from those first prostate symptoms: frequent need to urinate at night, delayed flow of urine, and difficulty initiating and stopping urination. It is used in tincture, 5 drops three times a day in some water. Other acute prostatitis cases can respond to Pulsatilla, Belladonna and Ferrum Phos., according to the clinical picture presented. Other more chronic remedies are Selenium (especially with impotence and erection disturbances), Thuja, Equisetum and Calc. flor, or in more advanced stages with formation of hard benign tumors, deep-working remedies like Conium. Everyone may benefit from zinc supplements (about 50 mg daily) as well as pumpkin seeds, which are excellent for prostate function.

### 2. Mental symptoms

One of the phenomena of old age is the poor short-term memory.  Of course, CFIDS patients, Alzheimer's patients and patients with immune-suppressed conditions like AIDS also know too well the signs of this early dementia. "Where did I put that knife down?" or "It's embarrassing, I have known you for 20 years and I can't remember your name." Sound familiar? Many of us don't need to wait for old age or disease to get this embarrassed about our poor short-term memory.

Besides supplements like Lecithin (500 mg, twice a day), many homeopathic remedies can be given according to the clinical picture. There is Baryta Carb., a good remedy for elderly people, especially following a stroke.  Aluminum is another memory-loss remedy, while an Anacardium candidate cannot remember the names of his friends. Glonoin forgets the streets he knows well, while a Nat. Mur. person is overcome with grief because he cannot remember the story he started to tell.

Other mental changes can happen with elderly people. Some become careless, worn-out, indifferent to their family members, sharp tongued and unsympathetic to others. They prefer to be left alone, taciturn with a stiff upper lip and crossed legs. It is a perfect picture for Sepia, which brings to the person and family a new lease on life.

Others start cursing, saying unpleasant things to their family. It is as if they have a split personality, not being able to control that other being in them that is raging and violent. Anacardium will bring much relief.

And everyone knows someone in their family who has become anxious and full of fears as they age. This person becomes obsessive compulsive, has a great fear of death, disease and contracting illness. They are overly tired and sleep badly because their restless mind keeps them up. They test your patience because they want everything extremely neat and in an exact order. Welcome to Mr. Arsenicum!

Many more mental pictures can be painted of the elderly, too many to mention. But it is wonderful to know that many harmless remedies exist to correct the mental deviations so often suffered by elderly.

### 3. Urinary Problems

We already mentioned prostate problems for the men. But another nightmare of aging is the loss of bladder control. The ·urine escapes involuntarily when laughing, running or coughing, or the bladder feels full, not relieved by urination. Equisetum or horsetail tincture is indicated for all those cases (5 drops three times a day). It is a wonderful kidney regulator, for elderly as well as young children suffering from enuresis or bedwetting. It will help the MS (multiple sclerosis) patient with his or her incontinence as well. Other excellent remedies for loss of bladder control are Gelsemium and Causticum, usually added to the Equisetum. How many elderly suffer from dropping of their

bladder or uterus (called prolapsed bladder or uterus)?    Often
Sepia is of help.

### 4. Circulatory Problems

Many elderly people have consulted me for heart
palpitations and nothing abnormal could be found on any of their
tests. Others always felt tired when walking or going uphill,
especially on windy days.  They experienced a pain which they
described as "if someone reached into my chest and squeezed my
heart."  Crataegus tincture is the heart tonic so many patients get
relief from, while Cactus will neutralize this sharp pain.

Others lose sleep because of "charley horses" or
continuous cramping in their legs the moment they go to bed.
While Calcium (1,000 mg) and Magnesium (2,000 mg) often help,
these cramps disappear forever if the right potency of Calc. Carb.
and Mag. Phos. (usually 6C or LM) are found by the
homeopathic physician.  I already mentioned Sulphur, which
cured one of my elderly patients who, after experiencing burning
feet for more than four years, came to me when nothing else
helped.

Apoplexy or strokes are other feared conditions.    Yet
Arnica 30C  given after these events is a most valuable remedy,
together with proper diet.  During the attack the homeopath has
several remedies at his disposal, according to the clinical picture:
Phosphorus, Opium, Ferrum Phos., etc. If there is paralysis on the
right side: Causticum 30C; on the left side: Arnica or Lachesis 30C.
In neurology we speak also of T.I.A.'s or Transient Ischemic
Attacks, in which there is a transitory (sometimes seconds-long)
vascular event.  They can possibly be precursors of stroke and
usually, a baby aspirin a day is advised.  There are some valuable
homeopathic remedies such as Kali-Mur, Crotalus or Lachesis.
Let your homeopathic physician make the decision!

# CHAPTER ELEVEN

## PRACTICAL TREATMENT PROGRAMS AND EMERGENCIES

*"As long as man is capable of believing that diabetes is disease, he will be insane in medicine. His mind is only directed toward the results of disease."*

-- J.T. Kent, M.D.

In the beginning of my career, I was a doctor doing house calls. Winter or summer, day or night, my patients could count on me any hour of the day or night. It was hard work, but rewarding. I was part of the family, greeted with friendship and respect, and patients never had to worry if a severe disease was going to strike their loved ones without proper and immediate care. Of course, there were also times that I attended a patient who was simply drunk. And I remember a patient who got me out of bed because her boyfriend's condom broke and she was afraid that she would become pregnant.

Here in the U.S. there are no domestic physicians any more, at least not in the big cities, and the burden goes to the ambulance service. How much anxiety has this created? Parents panic when their child gets a high fever around midnight, not knowing what to do. Mothers run around with children in their arms at 3 a.m. because they're teething and require constant carrying to be comforted. Household emergencies abound, and are unpredictable. You smashed your finger because your child slammed the car door on your hand. Your three year-old burned his fingers on the stove while exploring the kitchen.

This chapter will give you the answers to help you deal with these unexpected events. Ideally a good homeopathic doctor will teach you more about these pearls of wisdom. As you get acquainted with the power of homeopathy in acute situations, your confidence grows. Although this information will never replace the true physician, what it can do is give you another resource for those sudden, unexpected and sometimes unpleasant situations.

## The Household Homeopathic Kit: Your Domestic Physician

While waiting for the doctor, you can become an active part of the first line of defense. At your disposal are gentle, friendly remedies, promising and delivering comfort and solace. Let's open our homeopathic home kit and see what we can find in it.

All of the following remedies should be used in a potency of 30C. I already explained in Chapter Nine how to use them: take either three pellets twice a day, or dissolve one pellet in water and then sip from it over a period of 24 hours. Often the fast, gentle action of these homeopathic remedies will stun and surprise you. I know of no better way of being introduced to homeopathy than to see it working in daily, small incidents. Be aware of short-term aggravations and how to deal with them. Chapter Nine clearly explains this to you.

### *Arnica Montana*

This little mountain flower has been called the "sportsman remedy," and with good reason! Any soft-tissue injury requires Arnica: sprains, getting hit either in a game or accident, spontaneous bruising, falls, traumas, even flu symptoms where you feel like you have been "run over by a truck." It will give relief after you've worked a whole day in the yard and you feel that your back is "broken." Or after you have simply overused your vocal cords singing away at your school reunion. Or after you helped your friend move to another place and lifting all that furniture has left you sore and bruised.

Arnica is the first remedy to use after a blow to the head, in the initial stage of a stroke (it will stop bleeding and absorb blood), or trauma to the eyeball. Watch out when the patient says that "nothing is wrong with me" immediately after a trauma: this surely will indicate the necessity of this remedy. Arnica 30C, three pellets twice a day or used in water (see Chapter Nine), will bring miraculous relief. The effect of Arnica on old injuries is also truly remarkable. It will stimulate healing caused by traumas years ago. In these cases use Arnica 6C. I know of no better remedy to start this discussion nor that better demonstrates to the newcomer the power of homeopathy.

### *Aconite*

Aconite is an excellent remedy for those conditions that seem to come on suddenly, like a storm. The fright, for instance, of almost being in a car accident or in "near death" situations, such as almost drowning, or having a life-threatening heart attack.

It is used extensively in children for the sudden onset of very high fevers, usually around midnight. Typically, the child has been playing outside that day, exposed to dry wind or has been sweating a lot because of the exposure to extreme heat. The child will be very restless, anxious and crying for cold water because of intense thirst. His whole body feels as if it is on fire (note: if it is only the face that is hot and red, this would require Belladonna, not Aconite). Often the child has a dry hacking cough.

### *Apis*

This remedy is made from the entire ground-up body parts of the honey bee. Just think about the effects of a bee sting and you know what you can use it for. Sure, you can use it for insect bites, especially for the sting of the wasp (while Ledum is better for other insect bites) but the real indication is for anything that looks red, swollen and gives a sensation of stinging, burning pain -- be it a sore throat, conjunctivitis, cystitis with negative culture or while waiting for the result of the culture and premenstrual water retention.  It is the number one remedy for sudden hives (as in an allergic reaction to certain foods, for instance, strawberries).

### Arsenicum

This remedy is probably one of the most useful for children and adults alike.  I would never leave for a trip without it.  It has saved the vacations of thousands of people who have used it.  It is the #1 remedy for traveler's diarrhea.  If you dissolve one pellet in 4 oz. of water and sip from it every half an hour, you will see the discomfort disappear that same day, and the symptoms will not return. Numerous are the anecdotes I could relate about this remedy.  I remember being in Mexico at a tennis camp when I saw my teacher disappearing on a regular, sudden basis.  I suspected Montezuma's revenge and indeed, in spite of anti-amoebae medications, he had been suffering from these bouts of diarrhea for the last week.  When I suggested that he sip from this glass of water with a tiny pellet in it, he was not instantly agreeable. But to his amazement after a couple of sips his discomfort disappeared and before I left he insisted that I give him the rest of the Arsenicum.

Arsenicum is also the first remedy to give to victims of food poisoning.  Often we read in the newspapers of outbreaks of food poisoning due to infected and undercooked foods or for salmonellosis in chicken.  What misery this little remedy can avoid!

The next major indication for this remedy is asthma, especially when the attack is between 1 a.m. and 3 a.m., and one that is relieved by heat (warm drinks, heaters), by an extra pillow and by changing position.  The sufferer is very anxious, fearful, weak and restless.  It is wonderful to see this remedy calm the spirit and the body's labor.

Incidentally, Arsenicum 30C or 200C is also given to dying patients.  Their mind comes to rest and they die peacefully rather than continue to hang on to a lost, painful battle.

### Belladonna

The "deadly nightshade" has been very effective in otitis media, or infections of the middle ear, in children. There is a sudden and brutal onset of symptoms, with high fever (102-104 degrees F) and redness, but only in the face. There is an intense congestion (like a pool of blood) seen in the face. It is similar to Aconite, but Aconite involves the whole person while Belladonna only involves the head. The onset is usually after 9 p.m. when the child feels pulsing, throbbing cramp-like pains which start and stop suddenly. The child wants to be in a dark room and in silence, since noise, light and being touched aggravate the condition. They will scream before you can even touch their ear because of increased hypersensitivity.

### Bryonia

The best remedy for headache (especially right-sided) or for pain that is aggravated by the <u>lightest movement</u> is Bryonia. You can see the picture of Bryonia in the patient who tries to avoid movement, light and noise at all costs. He lies in bed with an anxious face, not even moving his eyes since that aggravates his piercing headache. He experiences intense thirst because of dry mouth. High temperatures usually start around 9 p.m. Bryonia is also the best remedy for broken bones as it will take the pain away and allows the patient further testing (X ray) and setting of the cast without much suffering.

### Cantharis

A great remedy for conditions involving the urinary tract, typically for the cystitis picture: burning sensation during and after urination, with increased frequency and urgency. While waiting for the result of the urine culture, one can start taking Cantharis 30C in water. Relief is immediate for the violent, piercing pains. If the culture comes back negative, Cantharis should be continued until symptoms disappear. At the same time, I would advise the intake of parsley tea, which is much better than the standard prescription of cranberry juice to help you alleviate the inflammation.

### Chamomile

Chamomile is a major pain remedy for children, for teething and ear infections. (See Chapter Three for the Chamomile Child.) It is also very helpful for colicky babies, but is contraindicated in nursing mothers.  In adults, chamomile is helpful in dealing with the withdrawal symptoms of coffee, for intense labor pains and drug withdrawal symptoms in general.

### Ferrum Phosphoricum

This is a remedy for "a lack of symptoms,"  for instance, fevers of unknown origin, with no other symptoms.  These patients feel weak and have a tendency to faint, either from weakness or from the sight of blood.

### Gelsemium

Gelsemium is the typical flu remedy, to address what we call the "Four D's": drowsy, droopy, dizzy and down.  This is how the patient feels.  Any effort to move is too much, he just lies in bed too weak to even lift his arms.  He is wiped out, listless and feels chills up and down the spine.  In spite of fever, he is <u>not thirsty</u>! He improves when he gets fresh air, and when he sweats and urinates.

This is also a great remedy for fear of the dentist.  Give your child a 30C dose before the procedure and your dentist will be grateful.  Gelsemium is also good for those students experiencing diarrhea because of anticipation fears before taking an exam. (Another remedy for these circumstances is Argentum Nitricum.)

### Hypericum

This remedy is great for any pain where nerve endings are involved: sciatica with sharp shooting pains down the leg, laceration of a nail (remember how painful it is when you crush a finger in a car door?), dogbites or other animal bites and splinters. Also a dose of Hypericum 30C is helpful after having a tooth pulled.

### Ignatia

I have discussed the effects of a "broken heart" on your health in Chapter Four. There is no better remedy to repair the sudden shocks that accompany grief, abandonment or hearing bad news in general. These patients sigh easily and feel a lump in the throat. They are highly romantic and idealistic; as perfectionists they are hard on themselves. However, it is hard to be rational with them while they are in their acute grief. It is truly a love-hate remedy working equally well to deal with the powerful and opposite emotions of love and hate.

### Kali Bichromicum

If you see green-yellow mucus with a respiratory condition, you panic. You may think that antibiotics are the inevitable treatment. You have a discharge of sticky, stringy mucus that starts and stops. You feel that your sinuses are stuffed up, and strangely, you crave beer although it aggravates you immediately. You must sit forward to bring up the mucus. Kali Bich. is often a great remedy for recurrent "sinusitis."

### Ledum

What Arnica is to bruises, Ledum is to puncture wounds -- the remedy of first choice, in fact. But Ledum often finishes the job of Arnica in traumas since it will speed up reabsorption of the fluids. It is the main remedy for a "black eye." It is indicated for joint pains which worsen with movement and heat, and improve with applications of cold. It is the number one remedy for insect bites.

### Magnesium Phosphate

Magnesium Phosphate is a big help for those monthly severe menstrual <u>cramping</u> pains, especially on the right side. The best relief is obtained by putting one pellet in 4 oz. of water, and sipping from it after stirring, every hour.  It is also indicated for writer's cramp and musician's cramps (as seen in violin or piano players, for instance).

### Rhus Toxicodendron

This is poison ivy and is also called "the rusty hinge."  At least that's how you feel in the morning when you wake up stiff all over, especially in the joints and lower back.  Getting up is difficult, but once you have walked around for some time you start feeling better.  In fact, you don't want to sit down for any length of time because that stiffness will creep up on you again. You can also be called the "human barometer" because you can predict the weather better than the weather forecaster on TV! When the weather is going to change (especially if it's going to rain or snow), your back lets you know in no uncertain terms that it's time to get out your umbrella.  All of the above symptoms are beautifully covered by Rhus. Tox.

## Other Practical Treatment Programs

There are many more instances where you can help yourself while waiting for the doctor to arrive, or call, or should I say, before you can go to the doctor for further consultation.  I have outlined some of the more common and some uncommon events in which you can apply homeopathic first-aid measures.

• Burns: 1st degree: Urtica Urens
      2nd degree (with blister formation): Causticum
      3rd degree: Cantharis

   Cause of burns:
         • overexposure to sun: Urtica Urens
         • hot water: Cantharis

- an electrical source: Phosporus
- a chemical source: Arsenicum

You can put one pellet 30C of the above remedies in water; give the child a little sip every half an hour and apply some of the water on the burn or use Calendula cream.

- Foot cramps or "charley horses" at night: Mag. Phos., or Calc. Carb. or Cuprum 30C

- Splinters: Silica, Hepar sulph. (especially if there is pus) or Ledum

- Acute sciatica:
    - left side, sharp shooting nerve pain: Colocynthis 30C
    - right side, with double bent over cramps: Magnesium Phos. 30C
    - sharp, electrical pain, following the path of the nerve: Hypericum 30C

- Bedwetting or enuresis: Equisetum tincture, 5 drops three times a day, in water (2 oz.).

- For an acute renal colic: Berberis 30C.

- For an acute cystitis, while you are waiting for the result of your urine culture: Cantharis 30C as well as parsley tea. Of course, it is quite possible that your discomfort will be over by the time the result of the culture is back and you will not need antibiotics. Remember we are talking about the "germ theory" and if the homeopathic remedy raises your vital energy, a germ will not be deterrent to your health.

- Heatstroke: followed by headaches: Glonoin or Veratrum Album

- Hives from allergic reactions to foods: use Apis 30C where there is a lot of edema or swelling; or Urtica Urens with less swelling.

• Worms in children: (symptoms include grinding teeth, voracious or canine appetite, picking the nose till it bleeds, biting nails till they bleed, itching ears [they bore their fingers in their ears], anal itching, blue circles around the eyes, a chamomile behavior [See Chapter Three] and large bellies):    Cina or wormseed is an excellent remedy.

• Delivery and Post-partum:  It is nice to know that there are safe remedies you can take to help you over some of the uncomfortable aspects of delivery.    To make labor easier, take Caulophyllum 30C during the last two weeks of pregnancy.  For the cramping pains: Chamomile 30C; immediately after the delivery, take Bellis Perennis 30C.  It will help you enormously to relieve the bruised, painful feeling in the pelvic area.  If there has been a lot of cutting (with a large episiotomy incision), take Calendula 200C, one dose twice a day.  For diminished secretioň of mother's milk, try Lac. Defloratum 30C.  For cracked nipples, try either Acidum Nitricum or Phytolacca 30C.  For intolerance to mother's milk, where the child vomits after drinking, try Aethusa 30C.   To stop the lactation when the mother wants to stop breastfeeding, try Lac. Caninum 30C.   For mastitis (breast infection): Phytolacca 30C.

• Rape: rape victims should see a doctor and counselor, but both of the following remedies will help in coping with this tragedy: Arnica is the first remedy to relieve the pain of bruises; next will be Staphysagria to help the victim overcome the psychological trauma.

• Recurrent colds or ear infections in children:   After your homeopathic doctor has determined the acute remedy (often Belladonna, Chamomile or Aconite), you need to reverse the tendency to this recurrent event.  Recurrent otitis media most often arises after antibiotic suppression which results in the "one earache syndrome."  Often Calc. Carb. in low doses (6C) or Merc. Sol. 6C will prevent recurrence of these attacks.  In Down's syndrome children, who are particularly prone to otitis media, excellent remedies are Baryta Carb., Baryta Mur., and Calc. Carb.

It is _imperative_ that you discuss this with your homeopathic physician.

For the simple otitis media without effusion (the child has fever, pain and sleeplessness; often fever can be absent because of a history of repeated antibiotic intake):

- fever: the child has a bright red face, is agitated, anxious: Aconite
- bright red face and sudden onset of fever: Belladonna
- bright red face, agitated, irritable, wants to be carried: Chamomilla
- no fever, pale, thirstless: Pulsatilla
- pale, thirsty, not better with fresh air: Mercurius Sol.

- Pregnancy vomiting: Ipecac or Phosphorus

- Pain from overwork, too much lifting: Arnica 30C

- Insect bites: Ledum 30C (first choice, even for bee stings) and Staphysagria 30C; for wasp or yellow jacket stings: Apis 30C; for severe allergic reactions to bee stings with difficult breating: Carbolic Acid 30C

- Poison Ivy: Rhus Tox 30C

- Hayfever: give one dose of Psorinum 200C, just before the season starts.

- Cigarette smoking: to reduce the desire for tobacco, use Caladium 6X, one dose as needed.

- Frostbite: Agaricus 30C

- Dental remedies:

  - Fear of going to the dentist: Gelsemium 30C; one dose an hour before the visit.

- For tooth pain after filling: Arnica or Nux Vomica are indicated. Take a dose of Arnica 30C before the procedure and you will need no further remedy.
- For an abcess: Silica 30C.
- Hypersensitivity to pain: take Chamomilla 30C 1 hour before the procedure.
- Excess bleeding after dental work: one dose of Phosphorus 30C.
- For pain due to cavities, before you can attend the dentist: Plantago 30C or tincture, 5 drops in water, three times daily. If there is pain because a nerve is irritated, use Hypericum 30C.
- For teething babies, nothing works better than Chamomilla 30C. Don't use Chamomile tea, as repeated intake of this tea will lead to an exacerbation of the symptoms.

• Fear of public speaking (this might also pertain to actresses and actors who have to undergo auditions, or students who fear to speak up in class): take one dose of Argentum Nitricum 30C before the event. Also excellent for fear before examinations, causing diarrhea.

• Pre- and post-surgical care: before each operation, Calendula 30C, one dose, will increase healing; postoperative bleeding as well as nausea and vomiting from the anesthesia will be helped by Phosphorus 30C; for avoiding formation of excess scar tissue or keloid, Graphites 30C repeated will help the best. Remember that you should always consult with your surgeon first when there is any surgical complication.

• Sun sensitivity: Sol. 30C or Mezereum 30C the day before exposure.

• Hemorrhoids: Hammamelis, Aesculus

• Cuts and scratches:

- Calendula will prevent infection and formation of pus in simple breaks of the skin
- Hydrastis: bleeding cuts, if they require stitches, they will heal much more rapidly with this remedy
- Plantago: an excellent remedy for infections after dental work because it has the capacity of "drawing out" pus and infected material -- it will also draw out foreign objects from the body, like pieces of glass or splinters
- Hypericum Perf.: for all wounds involving nerve endings, the pain runs up the course of a nerve (like in sciatica) or along a red line along the nerve. Excellent for injuries to the eyes and fingers.
- Ledum: for puncture wounds (swollen, not bleeding much) and insect bites

- Flu: There are some great flu remedies in homeopathy. Several clinical pictures are possible. You can feel drowsy, dizzy, down, depressed. You don't want to leave your bed, and even lifting up your arm seems unmanageable. You are so tired that you can't sleep and you are not thirsty at all. This is the Gelsemium picture.

If you additionally have muscle pains and deep bone pains, feel restless and bruised but not thirsty, Eupatorium is indicated. Another picture shows nightsweats, intense thirst, fever with chills, sore throat (the whole throat), foul smelling breath and increased salivation. This calls for Mercury Sol. There are other flu remedies such as Arsenicum, and Phosphoric Acid. No matter what "virus" causes the flu epidemic, a remedy picture can be found in the symptoms of the patient.

- Radiation treatment for cancer: Every unfortunate cancer patient who must go through radiation treatment suffers side effects such as suppression of bone marrow activity and the miserable diarrhea, nausea and vomiting. You can minimize these side effects with homeopathic remedies. While you are undergoing radiation therapy, take Cadmium Sulph. 30C each dose, before and after treatments; this can be repeated if necessary between radiation sessions.

• Nose bleeds: Phosphorus, Ferrum Phos., Vipera

• Premenstrual Syndrome: PMS is a curse for many women. Clinics "specializing" in PMS crop up everywhere and promise wonder treatments.  But most of these clinics, even if they use "natural" treatments, don't offer an approach that's appreciably different than the regular Western one. Typical prescriptions are natural progesterone, vitamin B6, and evening primrose oil. But these treatments offer little more than bandaid therapy, treating women as if they consist only of their menstrual cycles. There are many homeopathic remedies that fit the different aspects of PMS, taking into account, again, the whole person.

There are a whole complex of symptoms that go along with PMS. Not every woman with PMS experiences all of these. But there are homeopathic remedies which will address each one. The following is a list of remedies to take during the week preceding menstrual bleeding:

- Nat-Mur.: this remedy works wonders when a woman experiences irritability, mood swings, water retention, herpes simplex I or II outbreaks, mental dullness, and feelings of wanting to isolate herself, of rejecting consolation, of being offended easily, and being very sensitive to rudeness.
- Pulsatilla: this is helpful when a woman cries easily, wants to be consoled all the time, is moody and broods, goes easily from laughter to crying, appears capricious, but mild, is easy to convince and lead; or when she is very sensitive, easily offended, and anxious, and has an aversion to mental work.
- Sepia: use when the symptoms include being very pessimistic, averse to having sex, being indifferent to spouse and children, being irritated by consolation, rejects affection, has an urge to clean, lashes out at people with a sharp tongue and is irritated by contradiction, noise, light, etc.

For these PMS symptoms, take the remedy in a 30C potency, and take three pellets twice a day.

Besides the uncomfortable conditions brought on by PMS, many women also experience dysmenorrhea, or painful menstruation, with cramping ranging from bothersome to extremely debilitating. The following are some of the different possible remedies for painful cramps, usually the first day:

- Mag. Phos.: to be taken for painful cramps, especially on the right side, which start and stop suddenly; the pain is so sharp that the patient will double up, leaning forward, holding her abdomen with both hands. This patient will also feel better when she applies pressure and <u>heat</u>.
- Colocynthis: similar picture as Mag. Phos. except less severe pain and more to the right side
- Cuprum: to be given for violent spasms, beginning and ending suddenly, that improve with drinks of <u>small amounts of cold water.</u>
- Chamomile: this is helpful to the woman who experiences hyperesthesia to pain, often felt out of proportion to the seriousness of the case. There is some numbness and great irritability accompanies the pain.
- Ignatia: very sensitive to pain, with mental hypersensitivity; they are melancholic, sigh all the time and withdraw into themselves.

The above-mentioned remedies are by no means the only ones, but they will help most of the cases. The best way to take one of the above remedies is to put <u>one</u> pellet of a 30C strength dose in 4 oz. of water, let it dissolve, stir well and take a little sip every hour. Stir before each sip.

# Sports Injuries

Being an avid sportsman all my life, I have had my share of injuries. Many times, I have marveled at the ease with which homeopathy repaired the injury. I will discuss the more common injuries in several different sports, and what healing steps to take, including appropriate remedies.

### Tennis and Other Racket Sports

• Sprains and strains: what Arnica is to contusions, Rhus. Tox. is to strains.  Where the injury has resulted from an over-stretching of a tendon or ligament, use Rhus. Tox. 30C, one pellet in water, three tsp. only from this one cup.  Repeat the next day with one new pellet in 4 oz. of water.  This remedy is especially useful for strains caused by reaching up too high, as from pulling a muscle from an overly-vigorous serve in tennis without first warming up properly.

• Hit by a tennis ball in the eye: Arnica 30C or Symphytum 30C every half an hour, 1 tsp.  Consult an ophthalmologist to see if there is bleeding in the chamber of the eye.  A back-up remedy is Hypericum 30C.  If there is a "black" eye from a trauma, use Ledum 30C.

• Tennis elbow: a sore, bruised feeling around the "funny bone," or epicondylus.  Ruta, Rhus tox., Bellis  Perennis and Agaricus are good remedies.  Use one at a time in water for several days.  When one does not help quickly enough, try the next one.

• Sunstroke after a long match: Glonoin 30C or Belladonna 30C is the answer.

• Hit by a tennis ball in the genitals: Arnica for the bruising and the pains.  This sports remedy has done wonders.

• Sore shoulder (a bursitis or periarthritis humeroscapularis) from overextending your shoulders: Rhus. Tox., Arnica, Ruta.

### Soccer

Up to the age of 30, I was an avid soccer player.  I can remember the numerous hits against my shins with extensive bruising, causing a stiff beat-up feeling after the game.  Arnica 30C is a savior in this situation.  Rhus. Tox. is a back up remedy in this case.

Soccer is a game of kicking but also heading the ball.  This can be pretty painful if the ball is heavy and soggy from the rain, or if you head the ball wrong.  The immediate contusion or the headache experienced after this is helped by Arnica 30C.  If the headaches persist after some days, and the neurologist gives you a clean bill of health, follow Arnica up with Nat. Phos. 30C.

There is probably no other sport where you can get more sprains than in soccer. I remember the numerous ankle, knee and inguinal sprains in my soccer career. Rhus. Tox. again will easily resolve these injuries.

I also had my share of fractures. You do well to give Arnica immediately, even before the bone is set. After the bone setting and the plaster, give Symphytum. It speeds up the knitting of fractures and shortens the time of healing remarkably.

Dislocations and luxations will be treated after reduction with Arnica 30C. If you have nosebleeds from a collision during the match, use Ferrum Phos.

Tendinitis of the knee is a common trauma. If Rhus. Tox. does not work, try Anacardium.

### American Football

The medicine bag of the team doctor should be filled with Arnica for this sport. Football players constantly bump into each other with great speed and force. Every football player should take one dose of Arnica 30C after every game. They will appreciate the immediate soothing effect of this wonderful remedy.

Whiplash injuries occur in football probably more than in any other sport. The first remedy to use is Hypericum 30C for the first two days. From the third day on, give Rhus. Tox. 30C. The remainder of the injuries are similar to those in soccer and respond to the remedies listed in that section.

### Competitive Track Sports

"Coup de Fouet" or the "hit by a whip" refers to the excruciating pain in the calves of runners after excessive training sessions. Agaricus is the first remedy, with Bryonia as a back up, especially when the slightest movement hurts.

Cramps in the calves (also common in soccer), especially after excessive exertion, will be helped by Cuprum or Mag. Phos. If the cramps have a tendency to recur, Calc. Carb. 6C, three pellets twice a day for two months, will prevent this from happening.

There is another extremely painful injury to which track runners are subject: getting "spiked" by the spikes on another runner's shoes. In addition to being very painful, this type of injury is prone to infection. To speed the healing, use Calendula cream locally and take Ledum 30C at the same time.

Overexertion after excessive training often happens, especially in the light of special events like important meetings or the Olympic Games: Arnica 30C is indicated.

If you have blisters from a heel rubbing against a shoe or from running in new shoes, using Calendula cream locally and Causticum 30C internally.

Most of the above-mentioned remedies can be used in other sports for similar injuries: in boxing, skiing, swimming, basketball, golf, etc. The best way of bringing relief is always to put one pellet of the 30C potency in 4 oz. of water, dissolve, stir well and take a little sip every hour. The same cup can be used for 24 hours, after which you will make a new cup with one pellet again. It speaks for itself that you don't have to be a sportsman to benefit from homeopathic remedies for your injuries. You can have a tennis elbow without playing tennis or you can be unlucky enough to break a leg without skiing!

## Travel Kit for a Carefree Holiday

It always amazes me how unprepared people are when they start a journey. There is no doubt that a stress-free holiday puts your vital energy in top form, but small events can result in disastrous holidays. No one should ever travel without at least some well-chosen homeopathic remedies in their travel bag. If you don't need them for yourself, you can be a hero for your friends who may be in need of immediate care. Let's investigate the most important ingredients in your homeopathy travel kit.

Let's presume you make a trip overseas, and you inevitably suffer from jet lag. You can easily overcome this by taking Cocculus 200C, three dry pellets before you step on the airplane, and another three pellets upon your arrival. Over the next day or two, you can repeat with three pellets once a day, as needed. Do the same on your return flight. If you travel by car and someone suffers from car sickness, one dose of Cocculus 200C, one half an hour before the trip, will help overcome the nauseous feeling (to the great relief of the whole family). Some people have great fear of flying and come down with anxiety attacks and diarrhea. Take Argentum Nitricum 30C before boarding, and you will be surprised how well you feel.

Has your vacation been spoiled by the kids throwing up in the car because of motion sickness? Tabacum 30C, taken before the trip, will spare you this agony. Some people get dizzy just watching moving cars or from the sight and smell of food, and want to lie down: Cocculus is your answer.

The next remedy (I would never leave home without it!) is Arsenicum Album. This wonderful remedy has done more for me and my travelling companions than any other remedy. It is the remedy to take in case of travelers' diarrhea (Montezuma's revenge), caused by parasites or food poisoning. Make sure you have a 30C potency with you, and take it in distilled water, little sips at a time. Of course it is a good idea to drink only bottled water, by preference carbonated water. Nothing works better! It is always good to have some friendly bacteria (acidophilus) with you, as you will want to replenish your friendly bacteria.

Next on the list is Arnica 30C, which will cover most of the traumas you can incur. Also, take along Rhus. Tox. 30C for those sprains. While we are on the subject of pain, you might as well take along Hypericum 30C for any injury to the nerve endings: a crushed finger, a sciatic pain, a fall on the spine with numbness or injuries to toes, nails and coccyx.

For many people, holidays are the time for travel. Holiday time is often a time of overindulgence. Too many fatty foods, rich foods, sweets and too much alcohol will be remedied by Nux Vomica. Are you going to a country with lots of sunshine? Then don't forget your Glonoin 30C. I would like to add Bryonia 30C to the travel kit, for headaches that are worse with the slightest movements. If you travel with small children, take Aconite 30C along for the sudden onset of high fevers, especially after being exposed to drafts after sweating.

For headaches and shortness of breath experienced because of high altitude, use Carbo Vegetalis. Start taking a dose two days before your trip.

If you go to mosquito country, don't forget the remedies mentioned before.

The last item on your list will be Calendula cream, for open cuts and wounds. A cautionary note: <u>Never</u> use Arnica cream on open wounds!

You will be surprised how safe you will feel after experiencing the benefits of these little remedies. The golden rule is to start taking less medicine when you get better. If you feel excellent improvement, stop the remedy entirely. Repeat it only if symptoms come back.

So, to review, here are the contents of your travel bag:

Cocculus 200C---Arsenicum 30C---Arnica 30C---Hypericum 30C
Nux Vomica 30C---Bryonia 30C---Aconite 30C---Calendula cream
Tabaccum 30C---Glonoin 30C---Carbo Veg. 30C

It goes without saying that most of these conditions will require further help from your physician. But again, most of the above mentioned remedies will be very helpful even while under the care of your doctor. I hope this chapter encourages you to learn more about your own health as well as your health care system. I believe that, thus informed, you will feel empowered to take a very active role in yours and your family's health.

# SECTION FIVE

## ENERGY BOOSTERS

# CHAPTER TWELVE

## THE ENERGY SUPPORT SYSTEMS: DIET, TAI CHI, IMAGERY AND YOGA

### 1.  A Diet to Reach Peak Energy

The subject of nutrition is as old as man's search for food, but the science of nutrition is relatively new. Diet plays an important part in the studies and experiments of modern medicine.  The U.S. Department of Agriculture recently revised its diet guidelines, calling it the new Food Guide Pyramid (See Figure   5).  All the various important food groups are represented, but the trick is to make the right choices, especially quantity-wise.

But finding the right type of food to eat is not our biggest problem: finding uncontaminated food sources is. Newspapers and magazines are increasing public awareness about toxic contaminants, bacterial content and carcinogenic pesticides in most of our foods.  The bad news is that this increased awareness does not guarantee that even the most dangerous pesticides are removed.  Eating wisely seems to get harder all the time.  For a detailed eating and nutrition strategy, I refer you to my newly published book, *"How to Dine Like the Devil and Feel Like a Saint."* (Full of Life Publishing, Santa Fe, NM, 1993).

However, in this section, I will try to give you some <u>food for thought</u>, to guide you through the apparent maze of food choices, full of far-fetched diets, with vitamin uses and abuses alike.

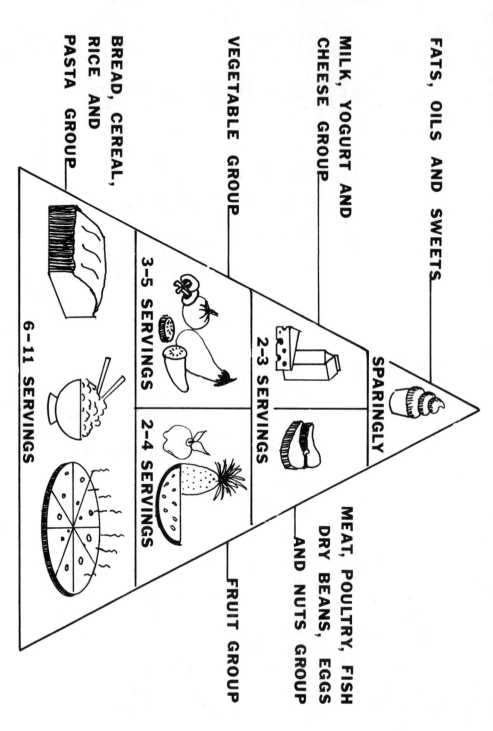

FATS, OILS AND SWEETS

MILK, YOGURT AND CHEESE GROUP

VEGETABLE GROUP

BREAD, CEREAL, RICE AND PASTA GROUP

SPARINGLY

MEAT, POULTRY, FISH DRY BEANS, EGGS AND NUTS GROUP

3-5 SERVINGS

2-3 SERVINGS

2-4 SERVINGS

6-11 SERVINGS

FRUIT GROUP

Fig 5

### Diet and Alternative Medicines

The subject of diet is not new to homeopathy. Hahnemann recognized how diet contribued to diseases when he stated in the 6th edition of the *Organon*, Par. 77:

*"Those diseases are inappropriately named chronic which persons incur who expose themselves continually to avoidable noxious influences, who are in the habit of indulging in injurious liquors or aliments. . ."*

This truthful statement won't be music to the ears of those patients who ask me on a daily basis: "Is it enough to take this homeopathic remedy or do I have to follow a good diet too?" When it comes to food intake, many of us abandon our in-born common sense. Often, because food supplies more than just fuel for the body -- i.e., comfort when depressed, a "lift" when tired -- we fool ourselves about what we are eating and how much. Have you ever heard a friend lament, "I am eating like a bird, but I can't seem to lose any weight"? I never believed this for a moment (with the exception of someone suffering from an endocrine illness). The proof is now out: a study published in the *New England Journal of Medicine* (December 1992), found that it was overeating habits rather than their "slow metabolisms" which were responsible for the study subjects' weight gains.

However, the homeopathic doctor takes these interrelationships much further. He understands the value of proper diet to combat diseases. When patients follow desires for certain foods, rather than choosing a variety of food which includes plenty of fruit and vegetables, he recognizes that these strong desires or aversions for foods are indicative of certain disease tendencies. Often these tendencies will be an important factor in selecting the proper remedy. He also knows that the cooperation of the family is a must to put a stop to the vicious cycle which prevents the return to normal health.

### Food: Medicine and Poison

Practitioners of modern medicine often speak to us in black and white terms: "Don't eat salt, don't eat sugar or sweets."

While these blanket instructions may contain a kernel of truth, they provide no insight into what Chinese medicine called "Yin-Yang" or the tenet of homeopathy, that "Like cures Like" -- that a substance can be either a poison or a medicine. Common sea salt has produced diseases like scurvy and hypertension, yet Nat. Mur. (which is sea salt) is a fantastic homeopathic remedy, used in many instances (See Chapters Two and Four).

This bipolar character of food substances is expressed in many homeopathic remedies as well as in the observations by acupuncturists 5,000 years ago. For the acupuncturist, each organ has a taste to its name: sweet for the spleen/pancreas; pungent for the lung; salty for the kidney; sour for the liver and bitter for the heart. This means that a certain quantity of a food containing that "taste" is required for the normal functioning of the corresponding organ. People put themselves in disease-promoting situations -- such as their eating habits and lifestyle changes -- and thus disrupting the natural balance in the body, depressing the involved organ under the weight of sugar, salt, etc.

Any food substance can heal or cause pathogenic factors, depending on the susceptibility of the patient. Even universally accepted supplements like cod liver oil can be rejected by allergic children: it can either produce symptoms or it can be equally therapeutically effective.

### A Good Diet is Common Sense

There is such a thing as common sense in nutrition: you don't have to be a specialist or go to medical school to know what is nutritious. Logically, if you can balance the body correctly through vitamins and supplements, you should be able to function normally. I often observe patients who take from 10 to 20 supplements daily but their health only gets worse. This decline is not due to deficiencies, but to the presence of toxins in the body, which impedes the absorption of nutrients. As usual, we tend to look at and treat the endings, not the beginnings.

In certain ancient tribes, herbal medicines were not given before the patient underwent a detoxification program, which consisted of purging, colonics and fasting. Only after detoxification was the remedy given. We can take a cue from this practice in our approach to disease. Otherwise, overeating and bad habits, having led to build-up of toxins in the different organs, will overload the excreting organs (liver, kidney, colon) and a supplement will be unable to change this. Only fasting, sauna, colonic hydrotherapy, raw food diets (especially in liquid form) and exercise will reduce the toxic environment of your body, clearing the way for a well-chosen remedy to work.

### Civilization and Nutritional Decline

Often, the simpler the diet -- as one can observe in little provinces far from the big cities, or in tribes far away from civilization -- the healthier the inhabitants. Napoleon Bonaparte's army could boast of having men of Herculean stature, with deep chests, large lungs and broad shoulders, hard teeth and enormous strength. Nowadays, it is hard to find soldiers of this stature in any army. Teeth are poorer, muscles weaker, endurance lower -- in short, the whole present generation is not very well developed.

Today we succumb to many gastronomic temptations and eat foods that please our palates, but that may be injurious to our bodies. A sad example is seen in the present Japanese population ( both in Japan and those who emigrated to the U.S.) who went from their traditional bean, vegetable and rice diet to the American hamburgers and fried foods. A sudden rise in degenerative diseases like obesity, hypertension, strokes, heart disease, colon cancer and rheumatoid conditions has been the consequence.

Fried, fatty foods don't contain much vital energy, and cannot be assimilated well by the body. The quality of foods that we grow are greatly dependent upon the chemical content of the soil, and since these foods must be grown on a commercial scale, agriculturists frequently resort to artificial feeding, another source of de-vitalized food. Processed foods make up too large a part of our diet, creating toxicity and malabsorption.

Today, we rarely see a pure, fully-developed lack of vitamins (avitaminosis), but we see many forms of sub-clinical hypovitaminosis (lack of certain vitamins). Orthodox medicine has found ways to correct these ailments through vitamin intake or proper diet. For instance, studies on rats have been performed in which deficient diets were given. If this was done for a short time, and the diet was corrected, they got well again. But is this the whole solution? If the laboratory rats were fed deficient foods for a much longer time, their lesions became irreversible, no matter how much their subsequent diet was corrected.

This is where homeopathy, because it looks at the total body system, can be more useful. Homeopathy, with its energetic remedies, will restore the unbalanced body. In fact, if the diet is not <u>excessively</u> faulty, the homeopathic remedies may repair the damage even without correcting the diet. I can only hope that modern medicine would do more provings in this direction. Unfortunately, from chlorine in water, to coloring substances in foods and alum in bread, the average person is consuming hundreds of toxic substances every day.

### What Is a Sensible Diet?

If we look at present and past food experiments, we discover to our amazement that "an infallible guiding principle directs us in the selection of food and drinks." Have you heard of the "cafeteria feeding experiments"? In these experiments subjects were presented with a wide variety of foods from which they could choose freely. This was done with small infants who selected their own foods over a period of at least a year. All children thrived on a diet of their own choosing. No bad effects of any kind were noted, and the diet chosen was not widely different from that recommended by nutrition experts.

This suggests that the organisms of man and animal alike do not need a scientist or nutritionist to tell them what to eat. Animals living in a state of nature select food according to their needs. There is no single general rule that regulates everyone's diet. This book has stressed more than anything the individuality of our species: there are different needs and requirements, and even different requirements for the same subject at different times.

Moderation is the key. We should listen to our bodies when we are thirsty or hungry. This brings me to the present biggest mistake in our daily diets. I don't know where it is written that we all need to consume "eight glasses of water a day." So many of my patients claim they are not thirsty but they drink enormous amounts of water for "cleansing purposes." At the same time, they complain about insomnia (because they have to get up four times a night to urinate), backaches, ringing in the ears, chilliness, fragile bones -- all characteristics of what we know in Chinese medicine as "kidney weakness." If you are drinking these quantities of water each day, your kidneys are suffering from an overload of liquid. I know of no other animal in the animal kingdom except the human being that drinks when he is not thirsty. You should drink according to what your body tells you: when you exercise and you sweat, you most likely will drink more. It's that simple. To force liquids on yourself and waterlog the tissues can just be as harmful as denying water when nature calls for it. To prescribe six or eight glasses of water a day may deplete the cells of needed chemicals and natural salts while the would-be healer is attempting to flush the kidneys.

Illness creates another hardship on the body, and yet we often urge those who are sick to eat. When parents push food on their sick children, they are neglecting what animals teach us. When animals are sick, they fast rather than eat. But there are certain rules to follow when you are sick. When you suffer from an acute illness (flu, diarrhea, sore throat, etc.) the physician and family should not refuse anything that the patient urgently desires. The delicate, subtle, infallible internal awakened sense determines food needs in conformity with nature. In most acute diseases there will be loss of appetite. In all such cases no abundance of food should be given until hunger returns. Overfeeding and wrong eating habits have predisposed to all sorts of disease both acute and chronic. Faulty management of the diet during acute illness is one of the chief causes of most complications and sequellae, the other main causes being overdrugging and suppressions. Is there any danger in fasting in acute disease? None whatsoever in children and young people, very little in other cases except in exceedingly toxic cases, particularly where there has been a history of overdrugging. Such people might be overwhelmed by the sudden release of stored food toxins and drug substances from the tissues into the circulation.

In acute disease you can apply several diet plans. Either water only till convalescence has become firmly established, or water with lemon juice, or nothing but raw, vegetable juices. Danger from constipation is greatly lessened by excluding the heavy proteins from the diet: meats, eggs, fish and cheese. If people were half as particular in watching their diet as they are in regulating their bowel movements, the health and vitality of the human race would improve to a truly remarkable extent.

The chronic sufferer, on the other hand, often desires the very food which has been the greatest single factor in producing his distress. The graver the condition is, the less the patient can be trusted to avoid his cravings. Humans are endowed with an accurate sense of when it is time to partake (or not) of food and drinks. During illness we are averse to certain foods and crave others. Cravings for indigestible things like paper, wood, and pencils indicates an inability to assimilate -- if the system is not assimilating certain things, it will crave that thing. A variation of this is seen in the "pica gravidarum" during the first three months of pregnancy where the mother will crave "weird" foods. This corresponds to the period in pregnancy where the expectant mother's digestive system slows down considerably.

As usual, we should faithfully obey the internal voice of our digestive organs, relative to the proper quantity of nutrients we should take in. This can be achieved by moderation, and when this is in place, it cannot be deceived by the cravings of a corrupt palate. During illness, the corrupt cravings voice will be more loud and clear, but for your own sake, always try to stay close with your inner feelings and the loud voice, guiding you in the sea of real food pleasures. Then you will see that the combination of homeopathic remedies and a balanced diet will yield results.

## 2.  Tai Chi Ch'uan: Restoring Your Energy

Eastern medicine has strong principles similar to those in homeopathy. Most of you have heard about the duality of Yin-Yang. They might look like opposites, but they are more correctly parts of one unit, an indissoluble duality. Tai Chi Ch'uan can be translated as "cotton fist," encompassing both softness and hardness, oppositions which are symbolized by the exercises of Tai Chi.  Every movement is circular and each movement will lead back to its opposite.  You go down before you go up, you pull back, then you reach out.  The movements correspond to the breathing pattern: breath out when sinking down, breath in when standing up.

One problem for the Westerner new to Tai Chi Ch'uan is the need for perseverance.  These small motions, done in seemingly tedious repetition, ask that the practitioner rearrange his life.  It is not enough to take a few classes from a master each week.  Neither will ten minutes a day be sufficient to approach the sheer power of the master.  Like anything else, you get what you put into it.

At first it is difficult to learn the sequence of these apparently disconnected movements.  But by merely following the teacher and performing the continuous repetitions, the mind will become one with the body. At a certain point, you won't have to think about the movements any more.  There is freedom of thinking.  Tai Chi also follows the law of acupuncture and homeopathy, where the energy comes from the inside connecting with the outside.  It is the internal energy, the product of breathing and thought, that is the driving force behind its short, powerful movements.

Unlike other types of exercise, Tai Chi doesn't require a special room, equipment or clothing.  There is also no sense of competition between the participants.  Only individual achievement is measured, each participant learning at his own pace.  It requires discipline of the body and mind to conquer the mystic strength of Tai Chi. Many give up, even several times, before finding the persistence to make Tai Chi a permanent part of their lives. Once that happens, the Tai Chi practitioner has found a way of inner relaxation and strength to offset the daily weariness of life.  But expertise can only come from long and hard practice. Once achieved, the practitioner's immune system has found a new, Herculean partner. His life will be better and longer for it.

# 3. Imagery or Visualization: Seeing with the Mind's Eye

*"A cheerful heart is a good medicine, but a downcast spirit dries up the bones."*

-- *Proverbs, 17:22*

All of us know those whose minds seem fixed on their suffering, real or imaginary. They are tough on themselves and even tougher on the rest of the world. They claim that they never feel good, are discontented, dissatisfied, and hard to communicate with. Even if they experience some improvement, they never will admit it. They are resigned (even attached) to their negativism and seem to be angry at everyone, including their doctors. It is hard for those patients to see that their anger and negativism will prevent them from getting the help they need so badly.

Some of these patients see themselves as victims of the world. They feel despair, hopelessness, paralyzing helplessness and an overburdening feeling of being victims of their past. Many of them have suffered tremendously as children and need all the help they can get. Some of them have gotten to this point because of drug abuse, sex and "free" lifestyle. No matter where the starting point was, these people need to start taking responsibility for their illness. Failing to do so only prolongs and contributes to their disease process.

Modern allopathic medicine is finally seeing the connection between the behavior and symptoms of human beings and the images they hold in their minds. Mainstream medicine now uses imagery to teach children with cancer how to visualize the "good guys" of the immune system attacking the killer cancer cells. Children play video games depicting battles between the different white cells and the "enemy." After the battle is won, the game then displays how repair can start through the work of other specialized cells. This should be one computer game on the obligatory school list. Children don't have to wait for sickness to strike before learning how to fortify their immune system through means of visualization. After all, school is where children typically catch most of their childhood diseases.

While Western medicine still struggles with the question of whether negative imagery merely precedes the disease or in fact influences it, ancient medicines like acupuncture and homeopathy have made the connection between thoughts and disease for many years. For these disciplines, the image or negative thought precedes the disease, and once established, will possess the staying power to influence and maintain the condition. Employing this view, we can't afford the price of a negative thought. Rather we should choose visualization to give intentional positive instruction to the body.

One of those commonly asked questions is whether there are existing certain types of disease-prone personalities, like a cancer type. This is an open-ended question for the allopathic community. Homeopathy has many more types. I already explained in Chapter Three the different types of personalities with their strengths and weaknesses. In alternative medicines like acupuncture and homeopathy, the negative emotion inevitably leads to disease, a course which can even be predicted. For instance, fears lead to weakness of the "kidney" which, in Chinese medicine, encompasses bone diseases, ear imbalances, hypertension, hair loss, etc. Anger and frustration leads to liver disturbance, insomnia, menstrual disturbances, eye problems, nail problems, muscle cramps, etc. There is a very real and hard price to pay for negative thoughts like smoldering irritability.

So don't use visualization only as means to fight disease, be one step ahead: use it to remove the daily stress from your life. Program yourself according to the Nine Signs of Health in Chapter One and you will prevent illness. Visualization will be successful if you use it to channel positive thoughts, and to prevent interference from feelings of disease and hopelessness. It will raise your natural defenses and lift your spirits. Visualization technique is often incorporated in hospital programs. Ask your doctor for more information.

# 4. Yoga, the Gentle Exercise for the Body and Mind

Yoga has been called the world's oldest and most effective way to radiant health and serenity. More and more people have adopted this Eastern philosophic technique and, much to their surprise, have seen wonderful results in restoring and maintaining their health. Yoga is attractive to the Western practitioner because it is gentle, requires no special equipment and -- always a plus -- provides immediate results as well as long-range ones.

It is no coincidence that yoga became popular 5,000 years ago in Northern India. Acupuncture started to flourish around the same time in China, which confirms the Eastern medical superiority around that time. Their principles are essentially the same: a quest for physical <u>and</u> emotional well-being. It is interesting how this aligns with the goals of homeopathy, and disputes the thinking of those who maintain that no other modality can be used while homeopathic remedies are being tried.

How yoga made its inroads in Western society is easy to understand. We have a society plagued by tension, competition, urgency and rampant degenerative diseases. The stresses of modern-day society have led to intake of tranquilizers, antidepressants, as well as a diminished quality of life. The saner individual wants to counteract this with a magic formula for inner peace, comfort and health: yoga. It has given its practitioner a way of reducing tension while gaining an alertness and a desire to tackle daily problems without feeling overwhelmed by them.

There are different forms of yoga, but the kind mainly practiced in the Western world is Hatha yoga with its physical postures and breathing techniques. Other forms like Raja, Karma or Bhakti yoga are often rejected because of mystical language used in the descriptions of their exercises. Nevertheless, the goal of any form of yoga is to return to the original state of the individual, where perfection existed.

The values of yoga are limitless. It follows rules found in other modalities like homeopathy. You can find the "Law of

Totality" (described in Chapter Six), echoed in yoga. Although certain exercises are aimed at reinforcing certain organs, its primary emphasis is upon general well-being. Yoga teaches that when the tree has healthy roots, no more sick branches will be present. This is totally different from the "branch-cutting" approach of Western medicine. Because the root is never restored, to the "amazement" of the patient and the doctor, the sick branch keeps on growing back, requiring yet another cutting job. After years of this suppressive therapy, the tree (human being) gives up and dies off. Yoga, homeopathy and acupuncture are designed to fulfill the Nine Signs of Health, rather than to give relief to a single local pain.

This "total" form of healing has only one goal: reaching a condition, a state for its follower free of desires, anxiety, fears, anger and yearnings. It will increase the peacefulness of the mind, leading to physical improvements like improved sleep, increased energy, more suppleness and weight reduction. It is hard to imagine that everyone on this earth is not willing to make yoga a part of their lives.

It was not my goal to give an in-depth study of the above modalities, like yoga, visualization and Tai Chi. Many excellent books have been written about these subjects. Rather, I wanted to draw your attention to the accessibility of ancient, non-invasive techniques. If you experience reduced strength in spite of following an excellent diet, this chapter should draw your attention to the fact that your job is not finished. Nourishment is one step, but restoration of what was neglected for such a long time is also critical. Without the help of the above-mentioned arts, this will be impossible. There would be many benefits if these disciplines were made part of our school programs. Can you imagine what impact this would have on the health deficit we now have in the general population? There would be less violence in children, increased attention span, less frequent diseases and especially, the seeds would be planted for a healthy, sane generation. Make yoga, Tai Chi and visualization mandatory for our children, and society as a whole would reap enormous benefits.

# CONCLUSION

*"Throw aside all theories, and matters of belief and opinion, and dwell in simple facts."*

-- J.T. Kent, M.D.

There is much that modern allopathic medicine can learn and is learning from homeopathy. Take, for instance, psycho-somatic medicine and one of the newer branches of allopathic science, psychoneuroimmunology. For almost 200 years, home-opathy has understood the importance of this relationship between mind and body and treated the whole person, prescribing for the totality of the symptoms.

Moreover, homeopathy can make fundamental contributions to show that when certain mental changes are induced in the body, they are invariably followed by physical changes. The experiments with laboratory animals performed so often by allopathic medicine are not suited for this work, as the mental and emotional attitudes of animals do not compare with those of humans. Homeopathy can induce mental changes in the patient lasting long enough to induce physical symptoms without damaging the patient's health. Without such material, psychosomatic medicine is doomed never to advance beyond mere speculation and guesswork.

The real pillars of science are *observation, deduction* and *provings*. Thousands have recorded the effects of poisons: it was

Hahnemann who observed and showed how to employ them safely and dramatically for the healing of the nations. Homeopathy has been the biggest gift to the health of mankind, but it has yet to become universally accepted. Homeopathic medicines are inexpensive, gentle medications. There is no need to destroy the environment so that we can produce expensive medications, full of side effects. Remember, all it takes is <u>one</u> root of one plant to supply the whole world and <u>generations to come</u> with its medicinal properties.

It is time for allopathic Western medicine to contemplate seriously what it is doing for chronic diseases. Most of the time, it performs bandaid therapy, fooling all parties involved into believing that a cure is established, when in reality only an acceleration down the road of disease is achieved. Not much has changed since Hahnemann alluded to this in 1842 in his *Organon*, paragraph 74:

*"Among chronic diseases we must still, alas! reckon those so commonly met with artificially produced in allopathic treatment by the prolonged use of violent heroic medicine in large and increasing doses. . ."*

The suppression of symptoms achieved by modern medicine will never contribute to the true restoration of health. Where do you think the rise in cancer, autoimmune disorders and epidemic diseases such as TB, gonorrhea and syphilis is coming from? Hahnemann in his genius expresses it very well (*Organon*, Par. 75):

*"These inroads on human health effected by the allopathic non-healing art are of all chronic diseases the most deplorable, the most incurable; and I regret to add that it is apparently impossible to discover any remedy for their cure when they have reached any considerable height."*

In other words, Hahnemann believed that modern treatment made the illness incurable.

In our attempts to treat these modern plagues and newly arisen epidemics, we will meet with little success unless we are able to trace them back to their original cause. That is the other grave, common error of modern medicine: it focuses on the endings, not the beginnings! Even when they do start looking at the true origin of disease (and I don't mean the presence of different germs), they will be confronted with an inability to repair it. Present medications are not able to restore broken hearts, loneliness, abandonment, despair and feelings caused by financial loss. All they achieve is a suppression of the vital energy followed by an array of side effects and addictions. Keep the Nine Signs of Health in mind and you will see that this suppresion has nothing to do with true health. All too often, present-day modern medications are heralded as lifesavers one moment, to be found later that they were actually harmful to mind and body alike.

Even though I believe it is important to recognize the shortcomings of allopathic medicine, I am not saying we should ignore the progress of other medical branches. This would be a serious mistake. No branch of medicine is so superior that it does not occasionally need help from another branch. If it were able to put its prejudices and arrogance aside, modern medicine could learn a lot from acupuncture and homeopathy. The strict principles of these sciences were the result of hundreds of years of observations made by eminent people like Socrates, Hippocrates, Galen, Paracelsus and ultimately Hahnemann who taught us that the remedy for a disease is to be found in the disease itself.

Homeopathy is not an easy science to learn. But no other medical science can contribute so much to restoring the health of the patient. I am suspicious of so-called "homeopaths" who establish a homeopathic practice upon an allopathic foundation, or practitioners who prescribe mixtures of homeopathic remedies in one bottle. This has nothing to do with true homeopathy and I would prefer an allopath to one who professes to be a homeopath, but does not know enough homeopathy to practice it responsibly.

We physicians have to stop patting ourselves on the back when all we have done is spend all our energy to classifying the patient in a disease group. Sure, a pathological classification will give important information: contagiousness, organ dysfunction and stage of a disease. But what the patient will need foremost is a weapon to remedy the vital energy which is at the core of restored and complete health.

Patients and physicians have much to learn about the mysteries of the human body. And in your search for health, to turn around the <u>critical condition of humankind,</u> you must be alert to finding the proper total-health approach. With the discussions and techniques in this book, you should be able to question a prospective practitioner to find out if your needs will be addressed as a totality of symptoms by this person. Look for a practitioner who is not afraid to keep studying and learning, and who is willing to learn from his or her patients as well. Remember, this journey to health and peak energy is a cooperative one. We are in this together!

# APPENDIX
## REMEDY ABBREVIATIONS

Acon.     : Aconite
Apis      : Apis mellifica
Arg-n     : Argentum nitricum
Arn.      : Arnica Montana
Ars.      : Arsenicum album
Aur.      : Aurum metallicum
Bar-c.    : Baryta carbonica
Bell..    : Belladonna
Bry.      : Bryonia alba
Calc.     : Calcarea carbonica
Calc.p.   : Calcarea phosphorica
Carb.v.   : Carbo vegetalis
Chin.     : China officinalis
Coff.     : Coffea cruda
Cupr.     : Cuprum metallicum
Equis.    : Equisetum
Ferr.p.   : Ferrum phosphoricum
Gels.     : Gelsemium
Glon.     : Glonium
Hyper.    : Hypericum
Ign.      : Ignatia
Lyc.      : Lycopodium clavatum
Mag.p.    : Magnesium phosphorica
Merc.     : Mercurius vivus
Nat-m.    : Natrum muriaticum
Phos.     : Phosphorus
Psor.     : Psorinum
Puls.     : Pulsatilla
Rhus-t.   : Rhus toxicodendron
Sabal.    : Sabal serrulata
Sep.      : Sepia
Sil.      : Silicea
Thuj.     : Thuja occidentalis
Urt-u.    : Urtica urens

# GLOSSARY

**aconite**: remedy given for sudden onset of whole body fever or fright.

**acrophobia**: fear of heights; an "ailment from anticipation."

**adrenal exhaustion**: overload of adrenal glands, located above the kidneys.

**aggravation**: a negative reaction to a homeopathic remedy. See also similar and dissimilar.

**agoraphobia**: fear of venturing outside one's house; fear of public places. An "ailment from anticipation."

**allopathic**: practitioner of a system of therapeutics in which diseases are treated by producing a condition antagonistic to the condition to be cured (Western medicine).

**aphony**: inability to speak.

**apis**: remedy made from ground-up parts of the honey bee. Common indications are insect bites, and other stinging, burning pains, such as sore throat or conjunctivitis.

**arnica** montana: so-called "sportsman remedy," derived from a mountain flower, helps any soft-tissue injury.

**arsenicum album**: homeopathic arsenic, good for diarrhea, food poisoning, asthma.

**ataxia**: failure of muscular coordination, one of the consequences of marijuana intake.

**aurum metallicum**: the metal gold used as a remedy for "ailments due to business failure."

**avitaminosis**: lack of vitamins.

**bacillus coli**: gram-negative bacilli found in the intestinal tract.

**baryta carbonica child**: one of three important remedy types in the digestive classification; often sickly.

**belladonna**: made from the "deadly nightshade" plant, given for middle ear infections.

**bouncing phosphorus child**: a remedy type under the sanguine classification in homeopathy. Sensitive, intelligent, but lacks physical stamina.

**brainfag**: a condition in which the brain does not function clearly. May be accompanied by short-term memory loss, and is often a sign of distress of the internal organs.

**bryonia**: homeopathic remedy for headache.

**calcarea carbonica child**: one of three important remedy types falling under the digestive type in homeopathy. Physically plagued by intestinal distress and emotionally by excessive worry.

**canker sores**: ulcerations, mostly of the mouth and lips.

**candidiasis**: either a superficial infection of the moist mucosae of the body, as in thrush or vaginitis; or a systemic infection or endocarditis (infection of the heart muscle). Both are usually caused by candida albicans, a yeast-like fungus.

**cantharis**: remedy for urinary tract conditions.

**CFIDS**: Chronic Fatigue and Immune Dysfunction Syndrome, a complex of symptoms of unknown origin, characterized by lack of energy, susceptibility to various infections, and brought on by a seriously weakened immune system.

**chamomilla**: one of two remedy types in the choleric classification of homeopathy. Snappy and irritable, these children are often miserable.

**Chinese classifications (or prototypes)**: five groupings of the basic physical and personality types, each governed by specific body organs: **earth** (spleen, pancreas and stomach), **metal** (lungs and large intestines), **water** (kidneys and bladder), **wood** or **wind** (liver and gallbladder) and **fire** (heart and pericardium).

**cinchona**: also called Peruvian bark, the first remedy Hahnemann proved on himself; mostly indicated for intermittent fevers. Will produce fevers in a healthy person.

**claustrophobia**: fear of enclosed places.

**conjunctivitis**: inflammation of the conjunctiva, the membrane lining the eyelids.

**constitution**: the aggregate of the physical and vital powers of an individual -- his or her temperament or disposition.

**Crohn's disease**: inflammation of the gastrointestinal tract, with scarring and thickening of the bowel wall.

**Cuvier**: French biologist who classified animal life into four kingdoms: vertebrates, mollusks, articulates and radiates. A contemporary of Hahnemann.

**cystitis**: inflammation of the bladder, arising from a variety of causes.

**cytokines**: cells of the immune system that are isolated and turned into drugs to fight cancer.

**dis-ease**: in homeopathy, a state in which there is a decrease in the body's vital energy, making it prone to infection and illness.

**dissimilar aggravation**: a type of reaction to a homeopathic remedy in which the patient immediately experiences new, previously non-existent symptoms, indicating the remedy was wrong and should be discontinued.

**D.T.s (Delirium Tremens)**: a disorder caused by the withdrawal from alcohol in the heavily addicted, in which the person exhibits sweating, hypertension, tremor and delusions.

**Dysmenorrhea**: painful menstruation, with cramping and often heavy bleeding.

**edema**: fluid retention in the body's tissues, usually causing swelling and discomfort.

**Eizayaga**: Argentine-born homeopathic physician who uses prescriptions of 6C, 30C and 200C.

**EMF**: electromagnetic fields which emanate from electrical power lines and electrical appliances. Thought to contribute to sensitivity in phosphorus types; in Western science, suspected as causative factor in certain brain cancers and leukemia.

**emotional trigger**: one of many events which is emotionally traumatizing and which can set off a chain of events leading to dis-ease in the body.

**etiology**: the study of the origin or cause of disease, and the method by which they are introduced to the host.

**ferrum phosphoricum**: homeopathic remedy for fevers of unknown origin, among other conditions.

**gelsemium**: a homeopathic remedy given for an "ailment from hearing bad news," and for flu.

**glossitis**: inflammation of the tongue.

**Hahnemann, Samuel**: (1755-1843), the father of modern homeopathy, which he described in his several editions of the *Organon*, the 6th edition of which is considered the definitive version.

**Hashimoto's disease**: progressive autoimmune disease of the thyroid gland, most commonly affecting women.

**hatha yoga**: the form of yoga most practiced in the Western world. Combines physical postures and breathing techniques.

**Hering, Constantin, M.D.**: a prominent figure in homeopathy, who outlined several tenents, or laws, of homeopathy, among them that diseases should move from the center of the body to its periphery.

**herpes simplex I and II**: an acute infected lesion, often painful, caused by the new introduction of or reactivation of a latent virus. Eruption often occurs during times of physical or emotional stress.

**Herxheimer reaction**: reaction of the body upon intake of medications with fever, chills and discomfort, of short duration.

**homeopathy**: a system of therapeutics founded by Samuel Hahnemann in which patients are seen for the totality of their symptoms and diseases are treated by remedies (administered in infinitesimal doses) capable of producing in healthy people symptoms similar to those of the disease to be treated.

**hyperglycemia**: abnormally high content of sugar in the blood.

**hypericum**: remedy given for nerve pain, such as sciatica.

**hypertension**: persistently high arterial blood pressure.

**hypochondria**: in homeopathy, a person who has great anxiety and fear of death, disease and contamination. Not used in demeaning sense, as is usually the case with Western medicine.

**hypoglycemia**: abnormally low concentration of sugar (glucose) in the blood.

**hypovitaminosis**: low level or lack of some vitamins.

**iatrogenic**: a disease or illness which is induced by medication or treatment, especially in Western medicine.

**ignatia**: a homeopathic remedy given for an "ailment from hearing bad news."

**incontinence**: loss of bladder control, due to aging or other causes.

**infinitesimal dose**: extremely small concentrations of medicine used in homeopathic remedies, according to Hahnemann's theories in the 6th edition of his *Organon*.

**kali bichromicum**: remedy for recurrent sinusitis.

**Kent, James, M.D.**: a Chicago-born physician from the mid-1800s who followed Hahnemann's 5th edition of the Organon. Kent's present-day followers, called Kentians, believe in high-dose prescribing of homeopathic remedies.

**layer theory**: a method used in homeopathy to build a time line of the medical history of the patient. Also useful in predicting the course of treatment.

**ledum**: remedy for puncture wounds and insect bites.

**libido**: sexual desire or sex drive.

**lupus**: an autoimmune disorder, considered incurable by Western medicine, and frequently involving the skin.

**lycopodium child**: one of two remedy types in the nervous, air classification in homeopathy. These children tend to be bullies and have violent tempers.

**magnesium phosphate**: remedy for cramps -- menstrual, writer's and musician's.

**malabsorption**: condition in which malfunction of the digestive system prevents the absorption of nutrients.

**marijuana**: cannabis sativa, a plant whose dried leaves are ingested or smoked as a recreational drug; in Chinese medicine, thought to create "heat-dampness" in the body, disrupting the balance between the liver (immune system) and the spleen/pancreas (digestive system).

**menopause**: cessation of the menstrual periods, often accompanied by hot flashes, night sweats, sleeplessness, dry vagina, urinary incontinence.

**mercury intoxication**: condition caused by mercury dental fillings, leading to a variety of local and systemic symptoms.

**miasms**: Hahnemann's three classifications of disease. From the Greek, meaning "taint, contamination, pollution or stigma."

**mucosae**: mucus membranes.

**Murphy, Robin, N.D., C.Hom.:** President of Hahnemann Academy of North America in Colorado. Author of the most modern repertory.

**natrum muriaticum child**: one of two remedy types in the nervous, air classification in homeopathy; may suffer from silent grief.

**nosode**: a homeopathic remedy made from diseased tissues and discharges.

**nux vomica ("poison nut") child**: one of two remedy types in the choleric classification of homeopathy, often plagued by abdominal discomfort and constipation, and jealousy.

**otitis media**: infection of the middle ear, very painful and with sometimes sudden onset in babies and small children.

**palliation**: symptomatic relief of symptoms, as opposed to a genuine cure.

**pathology**: a branch of Western medicine that studies the essential cause of disease, practiced most often post-mortem, but also on tissue samples taken during surgery on live patients.

**periphery**: external organs -- skin, mucous membranes, excretory organs, vagina, urinary system, bronchial system, gastrointestinal system -- through which the body rids itself of toxic products.

**P.I.D.**: Pelvic Inflammatory Disease.

**PMS (Premenstrual Syndrome)**: a complex of symptoms ranging from bloating and breast tenderness to mood swings, typically occurring in the week prior to menses.

**polyposis**: development of multiple polyps on a body part.

**prolapse**: sinking of an organ due to a lack of muscle tone. Commonly seen in the uterus and bladder.

**prover**: a healthy person who tests a homeopathic remedy, and in whom the remedy will produce similar symptoms of the remedy.

**provings**: testing the pure effects of homeopathic remedies on healthy individuals. A single remedy is often given to many provers and in this way all the symptoms will be shown.

**PSA (Prostatic Specific Antigen)**: a new blood test given to detect the presence of prostate cancer in men.

**psora**: one of Hahnemann's three miasms, defined as scabies or the itch. Physically expressed by skin symptoms; emotionally by moodiness.

**psychoneuroimmunology**: a newer branch of Western medicine, which studies the interrelationship between emotions, the nervous system, and immune response.

**psychosomatic**: having bodily symptoms of emotional or mental origin. Often used as a dismissive term in Western medicine.

**pulsatilla child**: a remedy type under the cold, phlegmatic classification in homeopathy. These children are often spoiled, prone to recurrent colds and exhibit many symptoms in puberty.

**Raynaud's disease**: a circulatory disorder of the hands and feet

**rhus toxicodendron**: homeopathic poison ivy. Remedy given to deal with anticipation fears and attendant diarrhea.

**sensitivity**: in homeopathy, an exaggerated sensitiveness to stimuli.

**silicea child**: one of the three important remedy types in the digestive classification; pale, suffering from recurrent ear and skin infections.

**similar aggravation**: a type of reaction to a homeopathic remedy in which the patient experiences an exacerbation of existing symptoms, indicating the remedy chosen was the right one.

**similia similibus curentur**: "like cures like," one of the foremost laws of homeopathy.

**stomatitis**: inflammation of the oral mucosa, due to local or systemic factors.

**suppression**: refers to the removal of surface symptoms, skin eruptions and discharges from mucous membranes.  Refers to pushing symptoms inward, contributing to exacerbation of the underlying causes.

**sycosis**: also fig-wart disease; the second of Hahnemann's miasms, typified by appearance of condylomata lata (warts); has its origins in gonorrhea.

**syphilis**: the third of Hahnemann's miasms, a systemic malady that causes pain and infection throughout the body, and depression and insanity.

**Tai Chi Ch'uan**: a physical discipline from China, meaning "cotton fist," and encompassing the softness and hardness, the yin-yang of opposites, in its movements.

**T.I.A.**: transient ischemic attack, a transitory vascular spasm and possible precursor to a stroke.

**ulcerative colitis**: recurrent ulceration of the colon, characterized by abdominal pain, rectal bleeding and discharges of blood, pus and mucus.

**universal reactor**: a person who is so sensitive to environmental factors that he or she often has to live in a stripped-down environment and not interface with the outside world. This condition is also called environmental illness.

**urticaria**: hives

**yin-yang**: in Chinese philosophy and medicine, the concept of bipolar opposites being integral parts of the same whole. The yang energy is the more active; the yin more passive and calming. Together they balance and complement the dualing forces of nature.

# INDEX

## A

acidophilus, 82, 175
aconite, 21, 64, 122, 159, 161, 166, 167, 175, 176, 197, 206
acrophobia, 64, 197, 206
acupuncture, 3, 20, 81, 103, 120, 141, 187, 189, 190, 191, 194
adaptability, 11, 13, 14, 206
adrenal exhaustion, 33, 197, 206
aggravation, 87, 89, 91, 100, 103, 108, 118, 119, 121-126, 136, 197,
          200, 205, 206
agoraphobia, 32, 64, 197, 206
AIDS, 1, 2, 21, 30, 80, 101, 138, 143, 146, 148, 150, 154
alcoholism, 69, 149-151, 206
ambition, 50, 65, 68, 206
American football, 173, 206
anorexia nervosa, 62, 206
antibiotics, 13, 78, 101, 108, 112, 144, 147, 148, 154, 163, 165, 206
antibodies, 13, 145, 146, 206
antidepressants, 58, 66, 190, 206
anxiety, 31, 33, 35, 46, 67, 78, 87, 133, 136, 157, 175, 191, 201, 206
apis, 148, 159, 166, 167, 197, 206
appetite, 11, 14, 15, 32, 66, 166, 185, 206
argentum nitricum, 64, 104, 152, 162, 168, 175
arnica, 90, 156, 158, 159, 163, 166, 167, 168, 172-176, 197, 206
arsenic, 91, 92, 95, 197, 206
arthritis, 1, 30, 82, 92, 105, 113, 115, 126, 146, 206
asthma, 1, 31, 33, 75, 77, 160, 197, 206

tai chi, 179, 186, 187, 191, 206
taxol, 112
TB, 1, 21, 79, 89, 148, 193
teething, 49, 157, 162, 168
tennis, 160, 172, 174
T.I.A., 206
time-line, 87, 89-91
tinctures, 117, 118, 151, 152
tongue, 27, 29, 31, 34, 36, 50, 103, 122, 135, 136, 170, 200
toxemia, 81, 82
toxins, 33, 72, 73, 81, 182, 183, 185
travel kit, 174, 175
triggering factors, 4, 36

**U**

ulcerative colitis, 64, 82, 93, 146, 206
urticaria, 62, 206

**V**

vaccination, 5, 143, 147, 148
vaccines, 82, 83, 143-148
vaginism, 62, 64, 90
vaginitis, 64, 198
valerian, 151
visualization, 188, 189, 191
vital energy, 17, 22, 25, 32, 42, 58, 65, 66, 70, 120, 121, 122, 125, 133,
    138, 139, 144, 148, 153, 165, 174, 183, 194, 195, 200
vitamin, 149, 150, 170, 179, 183

**W**

water type, 27, 32
Western medicine, 9, 21-23, 25, 39, 41, 55, 69, 71, 72, 80, 102, 103,
    113, 114, 122, 124, 138, 148, 149, 189, 191, 193, 197, 201, 202,
    204
World Health Organization, 105

# ORDERFORM

Please send (   ) copy(ies) of the book

## "CANDIDA"
## The Symptoms, the Causes, the Cure

Unit price: $10.00
Postage: $2.50
New Mexico residents add 6.125% sales tax

Ship to:

Name: _____

Street: _____

City: _____ State: _____ Zip: _____

| Total purchase amount: $ |
|---|

Please send check or money order to:

**FULL OF LIFE PUBL.**
**PO BOX 31025**
**SANTA FE, NM 87594**
**FAX   505-982-4011**

# ORDERFORM

Please send (   ) copy(ies) of the book

## "FULL OF LIFE"
## How to Achieve and Maintain Peak Immunity

Unit price: $12.95
Postage: $2.50
New Mexico residents add 6.125% sales tax

Ship to:

Name: _____

Street: _____

City: _____ State: _____ Zip: _____

Total purchase amount: $

Please send check or money order to:

**Full of Life Publishing**
**500 N. Guadalupe St. G441**
**Santa Fe, New Mexico 87501**

# ORDERFORM

Please send (  ) copy(ies) of the book

## "HOW TO DINE LIKE THE DEVIL AND FEEL LIKE A SAINT"
### Good-Bye To Guilty Eating

Unit price: $17.95
Postage: $2.50
New Mexico residents add 6.125% sales tax

Ship to:

Name: _____

Street: _____

City: _____State:_____Zip:_____

Total purchase amount: $

Please send check or money order to:

**Full of Life Publishing
500 N. Guadalupe St. G441
Santa Fe, New Mexico 87501**

# ORDERFORM

Please send (   ) copy(ies) of the book

## "HUMAN CONDITION: *CRITICAL*"

Unit price: $12.95
Postage: $2.50
New Mexico residents add  6.125% sales tax

Ship to:

Name:_____

Street:_____

City:_____State:_____Zip:_____

| Total purchase amount: $ |
| --- |

Please send check or money order to:

**Full of Life Publishing
500 N. Guadalupe St. G441
Santa Fe, New Mexico 87501**